A WHOLE WORLD OF TROUBLE

A Novel

HELEN CHAPPELL

SIMON & SCHUSTER

New York London Toronto Sydney Singapore

SIMON & SCHUSTER
Rockefeller Center
1230 Avenue of the Americas
New York, NY 10020

SIMON & SCHUSTER and colophon are registered trademarks
of Simon & Schuster, Inc.

For information regarding special discounts for bulk purchases,
please contact Simon & Schuster Special Sales at 1-800-456-6798
or business@simonandschuster.com

Manufactured in the United States of America

1   3   5   7   9   10   8   6   4   2

Library of Congress Cataloging-in-Publication Data
Chappell, Helen.
A whole world of trouble: a novel/Helen Chappell.
p.   cm.
1. Sisters—Fiction. 2. Maryland—Fiction. 3. Mothers—Death—Fiction.
I. Title.
PS3553.H299W48   2003   813'.54—dc21   2003042512
ISBN 978-1-4165-7843-7

In memory of
Audrey Bayley,
who dearly loved a good scandal

ACKNOWLEDGMENTS

Oysterback would never have been chronicled had it not been for my erstwhile Baltimore *Sun* editor, Hal Piper, who published the doings of its denizens on the Op Com Page for nearly a decade. *A Whole World of Trouble* exists because my agent, Nancy Yost, and her assistant, Julie Culver, worked hard to make it happen. At Simon & Schuster, I've had the great good fortune to work with the wonderful Chuck Adams, Cheryl Weinstein, and Martha Schwartz. My old friend Sybil Pincus worked her detailing magic on the copyedits, for which I will always be grateful. I have been extremely fortunate to have such great editors and supporters. If there are glitches, they are mine and mine alone.

Lisa Foss, Susan Anderson, and Doris Ann Norris read the work as it unfolded, providing moral support on the home front. To them, and to the TeaBuds and Salonistas, my deepest thanks for being there.

A WHOLE WORLD OF TROUBLE

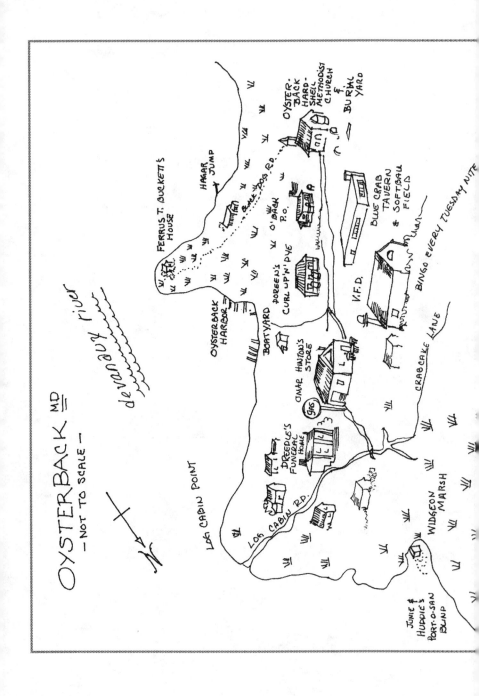

Sad to the Bone

I should have known that Momma would be late for her own funeral.

She'd been late for everything else in her life, so it seemed appropriate that she'd be delayed in death. Some of my earliest memories involved being hauled down the road by Momma, late for this or that appointment or lunch or meeting. I think that's why Daddy went the way he did, quietly sitting in the car in front of Doreen's Curl Up 'n' Dye Salon de Beauté. He died of waiting for Momma.

"Well, it's not really her fault," my sister, Earlene, said. "Wayne was trying to bring her ashes through the airport security, and you know Wayne, he gets a little excited."

"A little excited," I repeated, looking around Momma's house. The casseroles and floral arrangements were already piling up on the kitchen table, and the place smelled like a funeral home. Only we couldn't have the funeral because we didn't have Momma's ashes, thanks to Wayne, who doesn't get a *little* excited, he gets a *whole lot* excited. But then, Wayne hasn't been right since Vietnam, and he wasn't even in the military.

"Why the hell did Momma have to go and die in Florida, anyway?" I asked, peeling off my rain slicker. The house seemed strange, as if Momma would come through the door at any minute, fussing over the food and flowers, lighting up a Kool before she turned her attention to clucking at Earlene and me.

My older sister had already given up any pretense of trying to set Momma's kitchen in order and was collapsed in a chair, staring at a coconut cake some Methodist Women's Association lady had dropped off the minute she'd heard the news.

In Oysterback, a death is big news. A town this isolated depends on births, deaths, and criminal behavior for current events, and the definition of a good woman is one who has a freezer full of corn pudding and stringbean casseroles at the ready.

"Momma died in Florida because she was down there trying to get Wayne straightened out, as you very well know." Earlene was a martyr to the end. Her attention had drifted to a plate of cookies covered with foil. She eased the corner up a little and peeked inside. "Miss Carlotta Hackett's black walnut drops," she pronounced, helping herself to one.

I sat down at the kitchen table opposite her. "Well, I guess it didn't work, did it." I lifted a bit of Saran Wrap and peered at a Sunrise Surprise Pecan Jell-O mold. Evidently, Miss Nettie Leery had already come to pay her respects. With the tip of my finger, I swiped a pecan off the top and licked at the Cool Whip. "Just tell me what she was doing with that alligator, that's all."

My sister looked at me as if she were seeing me for the first time. Maybe she was just recalling that she swore, when last we met, that she'd never speak to me again.

"It was an accident," she hissed at me. "A terrible, terrible, most unfortunate accident, and I don't want to hear you say anything different to anyone, you hear?"

"An unfortunate accident with a Florida reptile? The damn alligator *ate* her, Wayne said!" I eyed Earlene indignantly. It was just like her to put a mealymouth spin on everything. While I considered Momma being eaten by a alligator somewhat romantic, all my sister could see was that it might shock the neighbors. Like you could really shock anyone in Oyster-back.

My sister pressed a corner of Kleenex to her lips. "Mind your mouth, Carrie," she muttered. "Momma was peering down into the alligator pit at Gator Gardens and she had a heart attack and fell in. It was an unfortunate accident. And that thing didn't *eat* her! It just *mauled* her a little, that's all. How can you sit there and talk about your own mother like that?"

I decided that if I didn't want to see Earlene have a full-blown case of hysterics, I'd best keep my mouth shut. Denial is a way of life for her. Otherwise, why would she stay married to boring old Romilar? Nonetheless, now that I had broken my neck to get here, she and I were fighting. It was just like old times. Call Vince MacMahon and get a Steel Cage Wrestling match going.

"Who told you Momma was eaten by an alligator?" she asked after swallowing a couple more cookies. Earlene is nothing if not nosy.

"Wayne, of course. He called me up three days ago and said that Momma was eaten by a sixteen-foot-long alligator at Gator Gardens, outside of Homosassa Springs."

"Well, isn't that just what you'd expect from Wayne?" Earlene asked the cake. "She had a heart attack, Charmaine, *a heart attack!*"

"Wayne said she fell into the alligator pit." She knows I hate it when she calls me Charmaine, which is my given name. It sounds either like some bimbo in a toga movie or some bimbo who lives in a trailer park. I became Carrie as soon as I could talk.

Earlene pressed her lips together. "I don't have to put up with this," she told a Tater Tots–chicken casserole.

"She was *my* mother, too," I pointed out. "I drove all night just to get here, and now you're telling me that Momma and Wayne are trapped at the Miami International airport? Who decided to have her cremated, anyway? No one asked *me*."

"Wayne thought it was more scientific. And cheaper than shipping a casket." She rolled her eyes.

While I was driving across the Chesapeake Bay Bridge, I swore I wasn't going to let Earlene get to me, and now I was in the house two minutes and already I wanted to kill her. Earlene can do that to me. And I can do it to her.

"This hasn't been easy for Delmar and me," my sister said, and burst into tears as she shoved a piece of coconut cake into her mouth. I watched the crumbs on her chin wobble up and down. I don't know how Earlene can be so thin or so blond. Well, not completely true. I know how she can be so blond. But thin?

I guess it was right then that it struck me that Momma really was dead, but it still didn't sink in, not the way I knew it was going to later. I'd been putting off dealing with the reality of it because I had to drive through some bad traffic, but now it was starting to hit home. Momma was not coming back. Ever.

With Delmar rushing to the rescue, what else could possibly go wrong?

"Why do I have to do everything?" my sister suddenly wailed. "How am I going to schedule a funeral without a corpse? We've got to get the church, and Parsons has to open a grave, and we have to plan a wake!" And then it really hit her. "Good Lord, people will think we're Unitarians!"

While Earlene cried, I got up and went out on the back porch to catch a breath of air. I also wanted a cigarette, and I knew if I smoked in the house, my sister would have a whole new round of hysterics, which I wasn't in the mood to deal with.

I sat down on the wooden step among the potted plants and lit a Vantage, staring out across the marsh to the place where the Bay met the sky. I noted that Momma's geraniums were planted in her old Wedgwood containers, the green and brown glazed ones that I can get fifty or sixty dollars apiece for from one of my dealers. That's one of the things about my line of business: you can't just see stuff as just stuff; you automatically put a price on it. Some people would say I know the price of everything and the value of nothing, but that's not true, not really. I just don't think it's a good thing to go around telling everyone about all the things you really care about. I don't like people knowing too much about me.

I gloomily watched a redwing blackbird soar over the hydrangeas, across the vast openness of the Great Devanau Marsh, where the yellow salt grass goes on forever. Oysterback is a sort of island, an extended piece of high ground threaded between the Bay and miles and miles of flat salt meadow. When you cross that bridge over Oysterback Creek, you come into a different world. Nothing out here but the mosquitoes and the blackflies. Driving here on the causeway, you watch the woods grow thinner and thinner until there's nothing but a skimpy layer of olney three-square grass and sky. A few narrow guts—shallow tidal creeks—wind their way in and out of the wet savannah. Here and there, cripples—small hammocks of spindly pines—dot the landscape, and if you get out of the car along the way to study a wading heron or a muskrat lodge or just the eerie, primeval beauty of this place, the mosquitoes and the blackflies will descend on you, covering any bare skin until it's black with biting insects. Some say that before the county began to spray the marsh, if you weren't careful, the bugs would pick you up and carry you away to make a blood feast out of your careless flesh. To outsiders, this place is not much, but it's home to us and we're used to it. But its isolation does serve to keep most people away.

The air was so gummy with August humidity, it was like breathing in one of Miss Nettie's Jell-O molds, maybe the

Marshmallow Fantasy she'd won the Jell-O Mold-Off with twenty years ago, back about the time I blew out of this town and swore I'd never come back.

I had, of course, but only to visit. Momma had a whim of iron, and when she said she expected you home for Christmas, she meant you were home for Christmas.

I still found it hard to believe that she was dead; I half expected her to come out of the garden shed at the foot of the yard and reprimand me for sitting on the steps smoking. Momma was dead against smoking since her first heart attack, even though she still snuck her Kools.

It was more than a sense of unreality that bothered me, though. I just couldn't picture Momma being dead because, well, Momma thought that the world couldn't go on without her. It was simply out of the question. I doubted that there was an alligator in the world big enough or mean enough to take on Momma. She simply would have fixed it with that look of hers, that cold-eyed Medusa stare, and the poor old thing would have backed away, muttering *sorry, no ma'am, it must have been a mistake,* before sinking into the mud to breathe a sigh of relief at escaping from that terrifying woman.

Out of the corner of my eye, I saw something glitter under the leg of the aluminum glider. I stuck my fingers under there. It was a bottle of nail polish. Rusty Red.

Suddenly, I could see Momma sitting on the glider in the cool of the evening, watching the sun set over the marsh as she carefully painted her nails for her trip to Florida. "I *had* to go get Wayne straightened out," she would say matter-of-factly.

And it was just as if she were sitting on that glider now, I could see her so clearly, looking at me over the top of her glasses, daring me to challenge her decision.

It was so real that I jumped, and burned myself on my cigarette.

But when I looked at the glider again, it was just the same old glider it had always been, and of course no one was sitting there.

I'm not a weeper like Earlene, who turns her tears into a grand and public production number, or a drama king like Wayne, who can make a paranoid conspiracy out of a sneeze. I've never been very good at displays of emotion. But now I felt as if something deep inside of me had been hollowed out and taken away, as if I'd lost a part of myself that I didn't even know I had until it was no more. That's when I knew for sure that Momma was really gone and this time she wasn't coming back.

Finally, my mother had met something bigger than herself: death.

"I'm sorry, Momma," I whispered, and suddenly I was crying silent, red-hot tears. I didn't know if I was sorry that she was dead, sorry that we hadn't gotten along better, sorry that I hadn't been there to say good-bye, or sorry for myself that I was all of a sudden an orphan. I was just *sorry*, sorry about the whole damn mess.

The first wave of grief was washing over me, searing and engulfing, like molten silver being poured inside my body.

So I sat and smoked my cigarette and watched the sun going down over the marsh and I cried. I was glad no one could see me, especially Earlene. The last thing I wanted was a pity party with her.

When I finished the cigarette, I ground it out in the soil around one of the geraniums. Then I stood up and went inside.

"So where's old Romilar?" I asked Earlene, who had polished off most of the pralines and was cutting herself another slice of coconut cake and holding it between her manicured nails as she slid it onto a paper napkin. She stopped long enough to give me a sideways look. If my eyes looked red and puffy, she didn't comment on it.

"His name is Delmar. D-e-l-m-a-r. He was named after his grandfather, who was a state delegate in Annapolis, if you'll recall. I wish you wouldn't call him after a cough syrup," she said resentfully. "It isn't fair and it isn't dignified."

I thought about Romilar, who looks like the Pillsbury Doughboy in a short-sleeved rayon shirt, and I winced. Years of living with Earlene and running the View 'n' Chew Sandwich and Video Rental Store has made him a chronic passive-aggressive.

"If you must know, Delmar left just as soon as we heard the news," Earlene added stiffly. "He caught a five o'clock flight from Salisbury, and he called the minute his plane landed in Miami. He's down there in Florida right this minute, tryin' to straighten things out with Wayne and Momma's ashes and all those security people."

At the thought of Momma's ashes, my sister began to tear up again, and at the same time she started to break off pieces of the coconut cake and stuff them into her mouth. It will never cease to irritate me how much Earlene can eat and still be as skinny as she is. I decided I would watch her to see if she went and threw up later. Maybe Earlene had been bulemic all these years and I just never noticed. That would certainly explain a lot of things.

"So, what happened in Miami that Romil—Delmar had to go down there and get Momma and Wayne?" I asked.

Earlene sniffled. "You know what Wayne's like. He'd made such a fuss about carrying Momma's ashes on board the plane that someone had called security, and they're holding him and Momma. Delmar will straighten it all out. You don't want to make a fuss at an airport these days. Even I know that. But apparently Wayne doesn't. I guess the urn set off the metal detector," she added uncertainly. "And that set Wayne off. And, of course, when Wayne went off, those security people went off, and, well, airport people have been so jumpy lately anyway that you can just imagine."

"Oh, Lord," I said, heaving a heavy sigh. "Maybe one of us should have gone down there when Momma died, instead of letting Wayne handle it all. And just who decided she should be cremated?"

Earlene straightened up, and her mouth got thin and hard. "In case you missed it the first time I told you, *Delmar* had to take time off from the View 'n' Chew to go down there! And it was Wayne who decided she ought to be cremated and went right on ahead and did it, before he even asked me! We couldn't get ahold of you! And speaking of that, you know, *you* could have gone down there. It's not like you have a real job or anything, living out of that van and driving all over the place looking for junk!"

"And do what? Haul Momma's body home in the van? Isn't it interesting that Wayne can call me on my cell phone, but you can't? And besides, I have a job! And it's a better job than standing on my feet all day, making subs and renting videos! I'm an antique trader!"

Well, actually, I'm a picker, but since I don't file for taxes or use credit cards or bank accounts, it doesn't really matter. Besides, Earlene doesn't know a damn thing about old stuff. She and Delmar bought everything in their house from Montgomery Ward, back in the seventies when they got married. It's a veneer and plastic paradise in shades of avocado and harvest gold.

Earlene tore the napkin from the coconut cake and scooped up the shaggy white icing with her finger, jamming it into her mouth. She eyed me nastily. "Now I remember why I swore I was never gonna talk to you again," she said around a mouthful of white mess. "Look at you! You're forty—"

"Thirty-five!"

"Thirty-seven years old. You have no home, no savings, no job—and no husband or children!" She regarded me triumphantly, as befit a woman who has a house, some money in the bank, a job, and two children—if you want to call those hell monster nephews of mine children. Personally, I think they're spawn of Satan, both of them. Loud, loutish good old boys with a worldview limited to TV talk shows and riding around in their SUV, four-wheeling on eight-lane highways.

And, of course, she also has a husband, if you want to count Romilar as a man and not a cipher.

"All you do"—Earlene was really getting into this now, her voice rising—"all *you* do is drive up and down the road, buying junk from people's auctions and yard sales and stuffing it into that old truck! That's no life for a lady! You're just an old hippie, Carrie, and you need to grow up."

"It's a good life! It's my life, and I do one hell of a lot better than you do!" I snapped back. "Wait a minute! *Old hippie?*"

"While you've been out there being an old hippie junk dealer, who the hell do you think stayed here and looked after your mother? It certainly wasn't Wayne or you! Oh, no! You both left me holding the bag!"

"Well, that was your choice, Earlene!" I was yelling now myself, but I didn't care. "Besides, what happened to Mike? I thought he was supposed to take care of Momma, not empty out all her bank accounts and run off with Reverend Claude Crouch, the Traveling Evangelist!"

Earlene's lips got thin, like they do anytime anyone mentions any one of Momma's former boyfriends. Since Mike had been a lay reader at the Oysterback Memorial Methodist church Earlene is so devoted to, his defection was a special sore spot. He'd run off with a tent revivalist and the Methodist Men treasury. Just another one of the no-account losers my mother seemed addicted to after Daddy died. My father had been a lawyer; most of these guys couldn't earn a living walking and chewing gum at the same time.

"You've spent your whole adult life avoiding responsibility!" my sister accused sullenly. "You weren't here to deal with that mess, either! Or the one when that idiot Dog got killed—or any of Momma's boyfriends!"

"I don't need this," I muttered, and slammed out of the house again. I was so mad at Earlene I could spit nails. But I was even angrier with myself.

The thing about death is it brings out the worst in everyone.

2

A Blast from the Past

I was happy enough to crawl into the back of my Econoline van and light another cigarette. Once inside, I was safe. Real safe, too. I had Dad's old 28-gauge Handi Gun—a short-barreled and very illegal shotgun—under the futon, just in case. I'd never had to shoot anyone yet, but on the road, it'd been useful a time or two when some jerk thought a woman alone was easy prey.

I mind my own business and I expect others to mind theirs.

At least the van was my own property, a place where Earlene couldn't yell at me. This is my house and my ride, rolled into one, the place where I live most of the time and the office from which I conduct my picking business as I travel up and down the Eastern Seaboard, buying and selling old stuff. I like to say I deal in antiques, but quite honestly, a lot of the stuff I buy and sell isn't really antique, even though I've got some big-time city dealers who pay me a good price for it.

You'd be amazed at the stuff people will pay out a lot of money for. I don't fool much with the high-end stuff, the formal furniture and the Chinese export porcelain and the antique silver and all of that; it's above my means and expertise.

No, I'm more into the sort of things that your grandmother had in her house, the kind of stuff you remember from your childhood. Mixing bowls, board games, dolls, dishes, magazines, model airplanes, that sort of stuff—maybe even a Howdy Doody puppet or a *Brady Bunch* lunch box, just like the one you took to school. Oh, it's hard to describe the stuff I deal in because it isn't anything too specific. But you know it when you see it in one of my clients' antique shops and exclaim, "Oh, I had this when I was a kid!" And your whole childhood comes rushing back at you in that single moment.

I look for stuff that my dealers want, and the stuff that I know that people will buy. Mostly, I deal in what they call "smalls," easily portable things that I don't have to sweat and strain to get in and out of the van; things I can pick up sell even more easily. Are you looking for an old celluloid dresser set or some McCoy mixing bowls? Papier-mâché jack-o'-lanterns, the kind kids had at Halloween? Apple corers and wall pockets and Roseville candlesticks?

I'm out there, prowling around, looking too. And because I know where to look and how to bargain, chances are I'll find it before you will. Earlene may call it junk, but it's expensive junk; I make a living.

When I'd gotten the call from Wayne, I'd just come from an estate auction in Roanoke, and my van was full of cardboard boxes stuffed with Blenko glass, ceramic wall pockets, and old hand-embroidered bureau scarves, which I was on my way to show to a dealer in Rehobeth Beach. I'd get there eventually.

I lay down on my futon, which serves as my bed and my couch, and kicked open the van doors to let some air through. The van generally smells like old stuff, that essence of must and dust, which I like, but tonight it seemed overpowering, even to me. Last night, I'd stayed in a Motel 6 near Annapolis so I could get a shower, watch TV, and sleep in a real bed. That would hold me for a while, so as far as I was concerned, I could stay in here until the cows came home. Or, as the case might be, Momma, Delmar, and Wayne.

Or, I could take off for Rehobeth tonight. It was only a couple of hours away, and it had been a long time since I'd been to the ocean.

I stubbed out my cigarette in a brass ashtray shaped like a monkey and thought about Momma some more. It beat thinking about Earlene. Thinking about Earlene is a dead-end project.

Among the many things about me Momma had disapproved of, my smoking ranked pretty low. Compared to my lack of even one husband and child, smoking was a minor vice in the canon of my mother's expectations. Daddy hadn't been dead more than ten months before she'd latched on to Dog Atkins, a waterman from down the road to Tubman's Corners, a man so far beneath her both intellectually and socially that even the minister had talked about it.

"A woman needs to have a man," she said as she glommed on to one of life's greater losers. As soon as they were married, Dog took up laying up on the sofa all day long watching the soaps and the game shows. His "bad back," he said, prevented him from working, while Momma slaved like a dog over to the office at Patamoke Seafood. But Dog's bad back never seemed to prevent him from riding up and down the road in the brand-new Ford pickup she'd bought him as a wedding present. When he wasn't on the couch, he was hanging around over to Omar Hinton's store or warming up a stool at the Blue Crab Tavern. I don't think he tonged up as much as an oyster once he got hold of Momma.

"You've got to have a man around the house," I heard my mother's voice saying. "A woman isn't anything without a man."

I almost looked around, but when you spend your life alone like I do, you get used to carrying on a dialogue with your past, as well as with what might become your future.

"Why didn't you find a man like Dog? He wasn't all that bad, except at the end," I heard Momma's voice saying, as if she were right there in my head.

Dog's bad back didn't keep him from carrying on an affair with Dawn Barlow, over to Tubman's Corners. Everyone in town knew about it a year before Momma came home early from work one afternoon and found them both on the couch. The dent Dog's prone body made in the old sofa was still there. You could see it now if you looked in the living room.

I guess Momma would still be turning a blind eye to Dog's sleazy infidelity if Dawn hadn't finally poured a glass of gasoline over him and lit a match. She got tired of him laying up on *her* sofa all day long, at least that's what she said at the trial.

Earlene and I referred to him as the Crispy Critter after that, but since he was dead, and Momma was a widow again, she didn't think it was that funny. "A woman is nothing without a man," she'd said again. "Men are like little puppies, and you have to treat them that way."

Despite Dog's long list of failings, Momma had been blind to his shortcomings. And I guess that's the real reason why I had to move out. I got sick of coming home from school and seeing ole Dog laying up on the sofa with his ugly old thing sticking up out of his pants, while he grinned at me as if he was God's gift to women, which, Dawn and Momma's bad taste aside, he wasn't.

Momma's little puppy needed some home training. Or a snip job. But I was grateful to Dawn Barlow for doing what I wished I could have done, what I should have done, if I hadn't been fifteen years old and scared to death of hurting Momma.

"The first prick I saw, but not the last," I muttered to myself. I might be single and childless and still a miss, but there's not much I've missed, oh no. Maybe that's *why* I'm single and childless.

"Knock, knock?"

I looked up to see a skinny little woman with a mass of bright red hair grinning at me. "It is I, Desiree Grinch, proprietor of the Blue Crab Tavern, four stars, *Guide Michelin*," she announced. Desiree talks like that, she really does. "I saw your van in the driveway and I came over with a plate of crab cakes for you."

Without waiting to be invited, she slid herself right into the van, a vision in a spangled Western shirt and tight jeans. Desiree dresses like a walking Christmas tree. She thrust an ironstone plate at me and gingerly looked around. "Can I sit on one of these cardboard boxes?" she asked, and plunked herself down without waiting for an answer, regarding me with her triangular green eyes.

"I can only stay a minute. I've got to get back to the restaurant," she said, taking my cigarette and giving it one long drag. "God, I miss smoking." She exhaled slowly and handed it back to me. "I gave up sex, drugs, and rock 'n' roll, but smoking is the one thing I miss."

I looked at the crab cakes. Two really big ones, stuffed with backfin meat, Desiree's best. And Desiree's best is heaven on a spoon. I dug around and came up with a plastic fork, and took a bite. That crab melted in my mouth, and I realized that I hadn't eaten since lunch yesterday in Richmond.

Desiree had commandeered my cigarette. Two plumes of blue smoke streamed from her nose. "When I went out back to dump the trash, I could hear Earlene yelling two blocks away," she remarked. "I'm sorry about your mother. I always liked Miss Audrey."

"She was different," I said around a mouthful of crab cake. I was practically inhaling it, I was so hungry. "But thanks."

Desiree angled her head the way she does when she wants to say something but is biting it back. I guess she sensed that I didn't feel like talking about Momma right then. "How are *you* doing, Carrie?"

I could tell she really wanted to know, too. Desiree and I go way back, even though she was in Earlene's class, not mine, at Oysterback High. She always had the biggest hair and a permanent cough from smoking in the girls' room. But from those humble beginnings, she took off, rather than sticking around, and when she returned many years later, it was with a pile of money and a great passion for Elvis Presley and gourmet cooking. What happened in those lost years, no one is completely certain, but there are hints of varied careers and multiple marriages, which give her a great deal of the sort of glamour you generally don't find in these parts. Not to mention a healthy stock portfolio.

"I feel like shit," I said finally.

"Of course you do," Desiree said, nodding. "I can understand that." With the long nail of one little finger, she flicked at her mascara. While I ate, she looked around, taking in my stuff and grinning. She drew a finger across the lip of an old slipware crock, as if she could divine its history with a touch.

"So, what's the news?" I asked. "What's the gossip?" Not that I really cared, but still, you never know what people are going to be up to around here. Last time I was home, a couple of watermen, Hudson Swann and Junior Redmond, had the bright idea of putting Old Man Hicks's PortoSan on four wheels and adding the motor from a John Deere lawn mower. It was going to be a portable duck blind when they ironed out the kinks, they said. They were tooling happily down Black Dog Road in their outhouse when the sheriff regretfully had to ticket them for driving an unregistered vehicle. It was a fun topic of conversation for a while.

"Nothing ever happens around here," Desiree pointed out

reasonably as she toked on my cigarette. "You know that. Oh, wait! In all the excitement about your mother, I forgot—Alonzo Deaver escaped from jail!"

"He escaped? The laziest career criminal on the Eastern Shore escaped from jail?"

"Big jail, over in Jessup, not the county detention center!" Desiree nodded so hard, her red curls bobbed. "Someone just came past the Blue Crab and told me this afternoon. It's not even in the paper yet, and of course by the time they get the next edition of the *Bugeye* printed, either he'll be in Mexico or they'll have caught him again, but—"

"What did he do to end up in Jessup? That's kind of big time for Alonzo, isn't it?"

"Well, remember that about fifteen years ago he messed with the wrong people and got himself a record," Desiree said cheerfully. "Then last spring the Conservative Christians Central Committee decided to have a fund-raiser, so they raffled off this .44 Magnum. Of course, no one minds if you want to auction off a shotgun, but there was quite a bit of hue and cry and unwelcome attention from the media over a big old handgun. Well, you know how humorless all those handgun people are," she said, grinning. "Alonzo bought about a hundred chances, and he won it. Now, of course, since he's got a record, they shouldn't have even let him hold the damn thing, but there were some big-haired political babes there from Baltimore, and some of those congressmen who have gunning shores over here, and all those pro-gun lobbyists, and they were all there to see the lucky winner get his prize, and do a grip and grin for the papers and the big shots, so they sort of had to let Alonzo at least stand there and have his picture taken with the gun and with them."

"Don't tell me!" I exclaimed.

Desiree nodded again. "Yep! Alonzo got his hands on that gun, and before anyone could stop him, he slammed some bullets into her and held 'em all up at gunpoint with the .44 he'd just won off them! He said all that money and jewelry in one place was more than he could resist, and he knew they'd take that gun away from him right away, so he wanted to prove his point."

"Oh, my gawd," I moaned, delighted. "He didn't!"

"Did! Right there in front of God and everyone! Cameras running and TV people and everything!" Desiree held up her hand, palm out, as if she were swearing in court. "It was the most embarrassment they've had since that state delegate from Santimoke County was caught doing the nasty with gay hustlers at the rest stop on Route 50!"

"Perfect! Just perfect!" I was laughing so hard I was spitting crab cake all over myself, picturing Alonzo holding up those self-important people with their own handgun.

"That's what a lot of us thought," Desiree agreed. "Even a lot of people who hunt and trap thought it was in poor taste to be handing out a .44 Magnum, since that Brockett kid was shot with the same model gun, maybe the same gun, for all we know—the sheriff we had then was no damn good—in that holdup over to Tubman's Corners. But, of course, the politicians have no sense of humor whatsoever, so when they finally caught up with Alonzo a week later, they went hard on him, and Judge Truax sentenced him to life. Truax said from the bench, 'That'll teach you to mess with important people!' Not that Truax was much good, either. They caught him takin' bribes from some of those real estate developers last year."

"Poor Alonzo! He wouldn't hurt a fly! He's a thief and the laziest man in the world, but he's not violent!"

"Well, we all know that. But we're just poor folks from down on the marsh. He should have asked for a jury trial, that's what.

I tell you, if there were a law against bad taste, every single one of those people involved in that raffle would be doin' hard time right now."

"When you're queen of the world," I said with a grin.

"When I'm Queen of the World," Desiree repeated, serious and reflective. It's one of the few jobs she hasn't held yet. She likes running things. "So," she continued, "Alonzo broke out. And I hope he keeps running 'til he gets somewhere safe. He ought to get an award for making all those rich, self-righteous assholes look like the fools they are."

We were both silent for a moment, thinking about Alonzo. We all went to the old Oysterback High School about the same time.

"You've really got this van fixed up nicely," Desiree finally said. "It's like a little house on wheels. I could use a van like this when I make my annual pilgrimage to Graceland."

Desiree's devotion to Elvis is fanatic. When you see the Blue Crab Tavern, you'll know what I mean. The whole place is a shrine to the King. I don't know if more people go there for that or for the food, although she's a legendary chef, which was the last career any of us who knew her in high school thought she'd choose. When Desiree's next-to-last husband died, she took her inheritance and bought a tacky old watermen's bar down the road and turned it into a three-star restaurant. The watermen are all still there. Desiree says they add to the ambience.

"It's amazing what kind of decorating you can do with Rubbermaid storage products," I said dryly. "Next month I'm being featured in an edition of *Lifestyles of the Poor and Obscure.*"

She snorted. "I like the way you put up all that shelving. Everything has a place. All you need is a toilet and a shower and you're set."

"I'm working my way up to one of those motor homes," I

suggested. As I pushed the last succulent bite of crab cake into my mouth, I noticed she was watching me, as if she expected me to collapse into a big puddle of craziness and grief.

Desiree quickly looked away, flipping through a box of old vinyl records, mostly early rock and rollers. This place is small enough with just me and my stuff. With another person, it's borderline claustrophobic.

"I almost forgot," I said. "I found something for you." I crawled around her on my hands and knees, moving some boxes and plastic bags around. It might look like a mess, but I know where everything is in here. After all, it's *my* clutter.

I put my fingers around a small bundle wrapped in newspaper. I felt kind of shy and pleased as I handed it to Desiree.

"I love presents!" she exclaimed, carefully folding back the yellowing *Miami Herald.* I watched her face as she exposed an Elvis whiskey decanter. It was a good one, too: fifties Elvis in a pink sports coat and blue suede shoes. I'd found it in a box lot at a yard sale in Jacksonville. I think it was one of the originals, made in '77, right after he died.

"Ooooh!" Desiree exclaimed, genuinely delighted. "Lookit this! I don't have one of these! Thanks, Carrie!"

She gave me a hug as she cooed and awed and played with the Elvis decanter; I could tell that she really did like it.

"Well, I've got to get back to the Blue Crab," she said with a sigh. "I left Ferrus, and you know what he's like—I forgot! I've got a new bartender—he's this teacher who moved into a boat down to the harbor after he didn't get tenure over to the college, but he's out of town this week. You ought to come over and meet him, Carrie. You two would have a lot to talk about, you living in your van and him in his boat—come on down, I'll buy you a beer." She paused, then added, "And he's not too hard on the eye."

I shook my head. "Thanks, but I don't think so. Not tonight.

I'm kinda tired." The truth was, I didn't want to leave the van, because I had a feeling that Earlene would get in here and snoop the minute my back was turned.

"Well, maybe later. You come on over anytime, okay? Any time, Carrie. Everybody would like to see you. And I'm always ready to listen if you need to talk, know what I mean? Sometimes, when you're grieving, you need to talk. And I know what Earlene's like," she added ominously.

I smiled, even though I guessed it looked as phony as it felt, all stretched and strained. "Maybe later, Desiree. Tonight, I just want to be quiet."

"Okay," she said, but I could tell she had her doubts about me.

I watched her gather up her Elvis decanter and her plate. With a last smile, she slid out of the van and disappeared into the night. Long after her shape was lost in the gathering shadows, the spangles and glitter continued to sparkle, and the scent of her musky perfume hung in the cooling air.

Long purple shadows of twilight were starting to spread across the village. I sat on the futon, smelling the late-summer scent of honeysuckle and low tide from the Devanau River. Oysterback. Two streets at high tide, three at low, someone once said. Just a little hamlet out on a piece of high ground in the marsh, a handful of clapboard and shake houses clinging to the edge of the river.

Every once in a while some painter or photographer rolls through town and oohs and ahhs about how quaint and charming it is out here, with the workboats and the skipjacks in the harbor and the faded old houses surrounded by grand old trees.

But they never lived or died here, which to my mind could be the same thing.

I thought about Momma, and the grieving hit me all over again, the knowing she's never coming back, and all the stuff we'd never gotten to say to each other that would never be said now. Worse, though, was all the stuff we *had* said to each other that could never be taken back. I cried myself to sleep and never felt so alone.

When I woke up a little later, the darkness had settled and I could see the lights going on in the neighbors' houses and hear their TV's and air conditioners humming in contrapuntal harmony to the mosquitoes and the deerflies. I lay back on my futon and stared at the stars I'd painted on the ceiling of the van, the silver constellations of the winter sky.

"Carrie? Are you in there, Carrie?" I heard Earlene's voice, peevish and tired, but I didn't open my eyes.

"What do you want?" I finally asked, before she could start pounding on the door and wake up all the neighbors.

"I'm goin' to the View 'n' Chew now. I left Jason in charge and God knows what a mess he's made of things. So if you want to go in the house and go to sleep, you go right ahead. We can talk more about things in the morning. Just don't you start goin' through Momma's stuff without me, you hear? I know what you're like!"

I could sense her finger shaking at me in the dark.

"No, Earlene, I'm not going in the house. I'm not taking anything from the house. I'm staying right here. I'm not getting out of the van, not now, not ever."

I could hear her hissing intake of breath, and then the silence as she pondered this. On the one hand, she liked it, because it meant that I wouldn't have unsupervised access to Momma's stuff, which she was certain I would root through and take all the best things behind her back, which is, of course, what she would do. On the other hand . . .

"What? You're gonna stay in this nasty old van right here in the driveway where all the neighbors can see it? What will people think? What will the church think? It doesn't look right!"

I gritted my teeth. "People can think whatever they damn well want to think. But this is my home and this is where I intend to stay. I'm not going anywhere. I'm staying right here in this van until Momma comes home."

And I meant it, too.

3

People Who Go Bump
in the Night

I had a dream that night.

I dreamed that I was at an auction.

But it wasn't just any old auction; it was outside, and the stuff was spread out across the empty fields, row upon row of it, as far as you could see. And the stuff wasn't the usual cheap crap you see at auctions, the teetering old bureaus and rolled-up rugs and boxes of dead people's chipped china. Instead, there was row after row of bright, shining globes of light. They floated in the air, just above the ground, in wonderful shapes and colors, glowing balls like small suns.

The auctioneer was going up and down the rows; I could hear his spieling and watch as globe after shining globe was knocked down to this buyer and that buyer, and some of them were people I knew, pickers who travel the same circuits. No one would ever accuse any of us of being pretty, but we are true to ourselves in a ragtag, missing-tooth, it's-a-long-sad-story kind of way. We just don't fit into regular society, that's all. We're different.

None of the other pickers seemed to see me. They were all focused on the auctioneer, who was directing their attention to one particular sphere of light.

It was about the size of a dinner plate, suspended a couple of feet over the ground, and it radiated a soft, warm light. I knew that I wanted that particular globe, that I just had to have it.

"Eighteen!" I heard myself saying, waving my number.

But the auctioneer looked right through me, as if he didn't see me, and he pointed to the hatchet-faced woman who stood to my left.

"Eighteen, eighteen, eighteen, do I hear twenny, do I hear twenny, twenny-one, twenny-one—" he says, like auctioneers do.

"Eighteen! Eighteen!" I'm screaming now, but he still doesn't hear me, and swings around to a hollow-eyed man, who nods.

"Nineteen, nineteen—this is a fine example of the craft, look at it glow—do I hear twenny-one, twenny-one—"

"I'm bidding, dammit!" I yell, which is incredibly bad auction etiquette, but I don't care, I just want him to acknowledge my bid.

But no one even looks at me. It's as if I don't exist.

"Nineteen! Nineteen! Do I hear twenny?" The auctioneer points his finger right through me.

"Twenty! Twenty! Twenty!" I yell, waving my card and jumping up and down. I want that sphere. That's *my* sphere. I must have it, because suddenly my entire future depends upon owning it.

"Sold to the gennleman in the red suit for twenny!" the auctioneer bellows, and I look over and see this guy with a smug expression reaching for my globe, my sphere, my sun.

"No!" I scream, and I yell so loudly that I wake myself up.

I sat up in bed, shaking and sweating.

It took me a moment to realize where I was.

I hate that dream. Most people I know say their nightmares involve being chased around by monsters or whatever. In my dreams, I'm always in pursuit of something I can never quite catch.

Awake now, I decided I needed to pee, so I crawled out of the van and made my way toward the house.

At night, Oysterback is so quiet you almost can hear yourself think. There was just the sound of the peepers and the crickets and Miss Nettie snoring next door, her gentle buzz drifting through her open window. No a/c for her. By the greenish glow of the street light down by Omar Hinton's store, a couple of hundred yards away, I could just make out the back porch. The glider looked like a big silver ghost, and something rustled in the branches of the old apple tree in the backyard.

Of course, Earlene had locked the back door. No one locks their doors in Oysterback. Why bother? Even Alonzo Deaver, the town criminal, knows where people keep their spare keys. Momma's key was under the Wedgwood geranium pot, just like always. Everyone keeps a spare key under a flowerpot in Oysterback, in case they go out to retrieve the Sunday paper in their bathrobes and accidentally lock themselves out.

I tiptoed through the darkened house, as if Momma were still alive and I didn't want to rouse her. I even avoided that middle step with the creaky riser as I went upstairs.

I didn't bother to turn on the bathroom light. After all those years, I knew where the toilet was. Like a bat, I could home in on it by locating the eternal drip in the bathtub.

What I didn't expect was that someone had left the seat up, and I almost fell in.

When my cold butt almost hit the water, I squealed like a pig. Then I let out a string of ripe curses as I grabbed the towel bar and pulled myself up from a narrow miss.

The toilet seat should have been a clue, but then again, I am totally clueless at three A.M. I finished up what I needed to do and started to stagger downstairs.

As I moved down the stairs, I could have sworn that I heard someone breathing. I stood there for a moment, listening to the house.

An old house is never silent. Momma might have been dead, but her house was alive with all the familiar sounds I knew from forever, the creaks and groans of shifting sills, the rumble of the ancient water pump, and the sinister gasp of the pilot light in the stove. Even the small, rustling sounds of the squirrels nesting under the eaves were familiar to me, as known a quality as the ancient tribal smells of musty wood, soap, and fried food that configured my childhood.

There it was again. A sound like wounded bagpipes, as if someone was forcing air in and out of a deep bellows.

Oh, my God, I thought. It's Momma's ghost, come back to haunt me.

Suddenly the thought was so real that I just sat right down on the creaky step, my mouth hanging open with surprise.

This is nuts, I thought, but I listened anyway, sitting very still. I wasn't afraid, but I did regret that my gun was in the van. Of course, you couldn't shoot a ghost, and I certainly wouldn't want to shoot Momma's ghost, if indeed it was her ghost and she had traveled all the way home from Gator Gardens just to haunt me.

I sat on the step, straining to hear the sound again. Naturally, now that I *wanted* to hear this alleged breathing, I couldn't hear anything. The house was suddenly as still as an Egyptian tomb. Not even the snakes that lived in the attic were doing their nocturnal crawl.

Then I heard it again.

Breathing.

If that's Momma, and she's come back from the dead, I thought giddily, then she *is* a ghost and there will still be time to ask some questions that had been hanging for years. Since I had walked in the door, I had felt Momma around me, just as if she were there.

The sound came again. A gusty sigh, and a creak, as if someone had rolled over on the old daybed on the sunroom porch.

A good imagination, as Momma used to tell me, is a curse. She thought I was cursed. "I don't know where you get all those ideas," she would say disapprovingly. "Men don't like women who think too much." That having of a man was the stamp that validated her parking ticket as a female. Maybe she was haunting the house looking for a man.

Creak.

I sat up straight and put my head against the railings, peering down into the shadowy living room. The dim green radiance from the road cast everything into shabby contours. Even a fuzzy glow couldn't improve the decor. You could still see the shapes of all of Momma's fussy bric-a-brac on every flat surface, and the lumpy old chintz-covered furniture didn't help matters much. It really looked as if it had been lived in, all right . . . and someone was still living here.

This time I knew it wasn't my imagination. There was someone down there, someone who was breathing. And it wasn't Momma's ghost. Only someone alive and suffering with severe apnea could make noises like that, sounding as if he were at the bottom of the ocean, being strangled by a vacuum cleaner.

I took a breath and tiptoed down the stairs. The snoring was coming from the Florida room. Through the glass doors, I could see on the wicker daybed a mound of something that had nothing to do with the decor. Whatever it was, it was where the snorking and snoring were coming from. To tell the truth, I was relieved that whatever it was, it was alive, and not someone from the other side come back to haunt the place.

Still, as Momma said, it's not the dead you have to fear, but the living. As I crept through the living room, I picked up one of Momma's brass candleholders.

Miss Peacock did it with a candlestick in the conservatory, I thought hysterically, as I crept across the floor.

The closer I got, the more the thing on the daybed began to look like it was more animal than human. Maybe it was a hibernating bear, or a St. Bernard, or God only knew what. Should I go get my gun out from the van? I wondered. No, too late for that.

My paranoid imagination went into overdrive. An escaped rapist–serial killer had broken in and was hiding out here while the police searched every other nook and cranny—that had to be it!

Hadn't Desiree told me that Alonzo Deaver had broken out of prison and was on the run? Cold comfort that Alonzo had never raped or murdered anyone, at least as far as I knew. In all likelihood, he had been waiting it out here in the dark for days, surviving on stringbean casseroles and Jell-o molds, marking time until he could make his big break for freedom by stealing someone's workboat and taking off for the Western Shore. God knows, an escaped convict could hide out in this house for days and weeks without anyone noticing. All he had to do was blend in with all the accumulated junk of a lifetime Momma had managed to cram into this place.

Suddenly, I smacked right into some of that accumulated junk. Someone had left a knapsack in the doorway between the rooms. When I tripped over it, the sound was as loud as if a cannon had gone off, but the serial-killer-rapist-bear on the bed never even moved. It just snored even louder.

Great, I thought as I leaned over the dark lump, trying to get a good look at the thing. I figured if I knew where its head was,

I could bash it in before it had a chance to jump up and grab me. Of course, it could have been faking it all along, just waiting for an unsuspecting victim to come along, someone it could take hostage.

Just as I got up on top of it, I raised the candlestick above my head. "Okay!" I yelled. "On your feet! Now!"

4

The Meet Cute

From beneath a mass of blankets, something stirred and rolled over, pulling a sheet up over its head.

"Go away," it said imperiously. "It's the middle of the night." Okay, so now I knew it was a man. Small relief. Before I could reply, it sank back into undulating snores.

Like a lot of things in my life, this was not going as planned.

I tried again, poking the lump with the end of the candlestick. "Hey, wake up!"

The man turned and rolled over on the bed, mumbling something I couldn't catch. "Go away," he repeated. "Lemme sleep, willya?"

"This isn't a hotel," I huffed, trying to sound as indignant as I could. For once, I wished Earlene were here with me.

"I figured that out. At a hotel, they let you sleep."

"If you want the bed and breakfast, it's down the road. This is someone's house."

"I know that. Now go away and let me sleep. I got back late and I have a lot to do tomorrow," he said from beneath the blankets.

"Well, you're not doing it here." One thing for sure, it wasn't Alonzo. He was much too calm to be Alonzo. "I'm callin' 911," I threatened, waving the candlestick.

"You do that, and while you're at it, tell Wesley Briscoe you're botherin' me."

"You know Sheriff Briscoe?"

"Ought to, he's one of my best sources. Now, go away and lemme sleep. If Miss Audrey knew what a fuss you're kickin' up about her lettin' me stay here while she's in Florida, she wouldn't like it, Earlene."

Well, that explained something. "I'm not Earlene. I'm Carrie."

You would think news like that would come as a relief, especially to those who know my sister. This guy just grunted. I had to be impressed with someone who wasn't scared of Earlene. "Who the hell are you?" I persisted.

There was a deep, regretful sigh, and he rolled over and turned on the lamp.

I blinked in the sudden flood of brightness and stepped back a pace. He sat up, peering owlishly at me. "You're *not* Earlene," he muttered.

"I should hope not," I said, snorting indignantly. A girl has her pride, after all.

He sat up, and I saw a man with gray-flecked dark hair and a beard. He was wearing a T-shirt that said SANTIMOKE COLLEGE, or at least it had in better days, many, many washings ago. He regarded me through squinting eyes as he pulled his wire-framed glasses over his nose and blinked.

I took a step back out of the pool of light and kept the candlestick clutched in my hand, just in case. He hooked his glasses over his ears and blinked again. It was as if his whole being came into focus.

He appeared to be about forty or so, a lean, wiry man with a deep tan and little tiny lines around his eyes. With the light on, in his glasses and T-shirt, he didn't look remotely dangerous. But then neither did most of those serial killers.

"No, you're definitely not Earlene," he repeated, still blinking at me. He pulled the sheet up around himself, but not before I had a chance to see his red-and-white-striped boxers. No thrill there. "Who *are* you?"

"I'm the other daughter, Carrie. The question is, who the hell are you? You scared the bejesus out of me."

"Oh, yes. Carrie—the one who travels." He sort of grinned, and I wondered what Momma had told him about me. Probably told him what a failure I am, which is what she told everyone else.

"And who might you be?" I asked.

He blinked again. "I'm Professor Shepherd. Jack Shepherd? Your mother said I could shower here and, uh, things while she is in Florida. She also said I could sleep here if I had to. And I had to tonight. I've been living on my boat, down at the harbor, and the waterman in the next slip to me went home and left his bait box open on the deck. In this heat, that salt eel stinks so badly you can smell it all the way up the road. I couldn't sleep with that stench, so I came here." He sat up, yawning. "Hell of a note, I tell ya. I've been down in Onancock for a week, researching indigenous folk beliefs, and if you don't think that's a thankless, miserable . . ."

Then I remembered what Desiree had told me, about the college professor who had lost his job and was working at the Blue Crab. This must be him; there weren't too many defrocked teachers hanging around this town.

Momma sure hadn't told me anything about him. But then, she and I hadn't been speaking a whole lot over the past few years. There'd probably been a number of her boyfriends I'd missed in all that time. Evidently, this one hadn't heard the bad news. But being an outsider, he wouldn't have.

I gave him the edited version: "Momma's dead." Now, I might think it's funny that Momma fell in the alligator pit and was chewed to death by a giant reptile, but it's not something I was eager to share with people outside the family, especially come-heres. I was kind of surprised, however, that Momma would take up with an educated man. Usually her boyfriends could barely read and write. That she would take up with someone about my age didn't surprise me though.

"So, Romilar—I mean Delmar went down to Miami to get it all straightened out," I finished, and it sounded weird, even to me.

When I got through telling him the company-and-guest version of Momma's untimely demise, he looked a bit shaken up, but not devastated.

"Gator Gardens," he repeated thoughtfully. "That's a shame. It's hard to imagine Audrey going so fast like that. She was quite a character." He frowned. "But . . . Gator Gardens? She died at a place called Gator Gardens?" He looked pale, more upset than I would have expected.

"Oh, Lord! I am sorry," he said, his voice choking. "Audrey was . . . very kind to me. But . . . Gator Gardens? It sounds so . . . *Pink Flamingos*."

"You mean the movie with Divine?" I gasped. The last thing I expected was to find someone sleeping on my mother's daybed who knew anything about one of my favorite movies. Much against my better judgment, I laughed.

"It does sort of sound like something John Waters would make up, doesn't it?" he murmured. "Poor Audrey, good Lord."

"Momma did sort of look like a skinnier Divine," I admitted. "The hair, anyway." Then it struck me how peculiar it was that I was standing there laughing with a perfect stranger about a three-hundred-pound dead drag queen when Momma was dead and not yet buried.

"Gator Gardens, Gator Gardens." Shepherd reached over to the end table and came up with one of those thin white notebooks like the kind reporters use. He scribbled something in it with a ballpoint pen and flipped it shut, as if he didn't want me to see what he'd written.

Intellectual types seem to have this need to write everything down, as if it doesn't count if they don't record both it and their reaction to it, whatever *it* might be. Clearly, this man felt he had every right to be there, and since it was the middle of the night, I decided to take my leave. Besides, I figured he wanted to be alone to think deep thoughts about Momma and death and other profound subjects.

So I said good night and toddled back to the van. But I did lock the doors.

5

Waiting for Death, or Someone Just Like It

Momma used to say that things would always look different in the morning, and they sure did. They looked a lot worse.

For one thing, she was still dead, and for another, I felt as if I had been ridden hard all night and put away wet, which maybe I had. Finding a strange man in your late mother's Florida room is not my idea of a welcomed thing. A man young enough to be her son! That bothered me especially, knowing Momma's interest in younger men.

Inside the van, it was hotter than the south corner of hell. On days like this, in high summer, without shade, it was like waking up inside an oven.

But it wasn't the heat that woke me up, it was a mockingbird in the magnolia tree, singing its little black heart out. The thing about mockingbirds is when they're awake, everyone's awake, because once they start in, they keep it up all morning.

I went in the house to wash up before Earlene got there and started in on me. Fortunately, the guy who had been sleeping on the daybed seemed to have disappeared. The only sign he had been there was the rumpled spread.

I guess I could have breakfasted nicely on Jell-O molds and slightly stale coconut cake, but all that Momma had in the pantry was instant coffee, and the milk in the refrigerator had gone off days ago. Coffee without milk is no way to start the day, so I trundled myself down the road to Omar Hinton's store, where at least I knew I could get real coffee and fresh milk, along with the latest gossip, assuming, of course, I wasn't the subject of it myself.

I decided to walk. I needed the exercise. But I locked up the van so if Earlene showed up, she couldn't get in there and snoop. I was pretty sure she'd go over my stuff, checking to see if I'd pocketed any of Mama's bric-a-brac while her back was turned.

See, that's the sort of thing Earlene would do, sneak up when no one was looking, so of course she thinks everyone else is just like her.

The day was starting to steam already, even though the sun wasn't even over the trees yet. A sullen gray dust clung to the trumpet vine that bent over the ditches, the way it does in a drought. It looked as if they hadn't had rain here in weeks, but there was enough humidity in the air to make me break out in a thin, sticky sweat as I started down the road.

I wasn't too surprised to see Miss Carlotta Hackett backing her '57 pink El Dorado out of her driveway next door. That car has ridden in more parades than John Glenn; every homecoming queen and Miss Oysterback VFD and Miss West Hundred Seafood Industry has ridden on the back of that convertible since 1961. That Miss Carlotta, Delmarva Poultry Princess of 1953, has been the guiding force behind each and every one of those beauty contests goes without saying. Ever since her own daughter, Tiffany Crystal, was killed in a drunk-driving accident on the night of her coronation as Miss Decoy Jamboree, Miss Carlotta has submerged her grief by devoting herself to beauty royalty, hairspray, and rhinestone tiaras.

I never made the beauty queen cut. Far from it. But Earlene

had been Miss Oysterback VFD in 1976, and had worn pink
tulle and sequins in the Fireman's Convention Parade in Ocean
City, waving from the back of that Cadillac like Queen Eliza-
beth. She practiced in front of the mirror for a week to get that
little wave just right.

Seeing me, Miss Carlotta touched the button that opened the
car window. A blast of arctic air and White Diamonds hit me
like a slap as I dutifully bent to greet her.

Her blond hair, an architectural marvel that would have survived a nuclear blast, bobbled as she leaned across the seat to
look at me as if I were a contestant who had belched during the
talent competition.

"I couldn't believe it about Audrey!" she bellowed, her
whiskey tenor booming over the roar of the Cadillac's a/c. "I
just saw her off to the airport last week! It just floored us all!
Your mother was the last person you'd expect to have a heart
attack!"

"I know!" I agreed, then waited because I didn't have anything else to say to her and never had. The Hacketts and I had
never been close. I hadn't liked Tiffany Crystal, either; she had
been a bossy snob, and a slut, if the rumors were true and I
think they were. Nonetheless, Miss Carlotta was a friend and
neighbor of Momma's, so I was polite.

She looked to the right and to the left, reassuring herself the
two-lane asphalt was clear of traffic. Then she leaned across the
seat, her acrylic nails drumming on the steering wheel. I have
never seen anyone so assured of her immutable place in the
food chain as she was, anyone so innately certain of her own
absolute right to exist.

"You know, dear," she confided in a voice you could have
heard halfway to Patamoke, "I hate to carry tales, but before
you came, Earlene was carrying whole cardboard boxes out of
Audrey's house!" The white cement confection on top of her

head nodded. "I'd count the silver and check your mother's jewelry very carefully if I were you!"

As I stood there with my mouth open, the window slid closed between us. She backed the behemoth out of the driveway and swung down the road toward her Monday appointment at the Curl Up 'n' Dye, leaving me in a cloud of dust.

I imagine the minute Earlene found out Momma was dead, she broke all land speed records for getting her big old Buick Electra over here from Tubman's Corners so she could go through Momma's jewelry. For Earlene, who has so much stuff, there never seems to be enough. She always needs more. A newer car, a bigger TV, more silverware, more trips to the Curl Up 'n' Dye, a yacht club membership. As if *more* could fill up the big empty hole inside of her.

I have a lot of customers like that, people who crave stuff, who covet and collect and hoard stuff, as if *stuff* were somehow going to make them complete souls. It never does, of course. It just makes them want more stuff, because the hole inside is bottomless.

I guess that's why I'm not married to stuff, even though I spend my life dealing with it. I've made it all a game. I don't take it too seriously and that's how I cope, if you can call what I do coping.

I had no doubt Miss Carlotta would be sharing news of Earlene's activities with everyone at Doreen's Curl Up 'n' Dye Salon de Beauté, and I couldn't have cared less. However, Earlene would care very much when it trickled back to her, as it would, that she had been spotted, through Miss Carlotta's dining room Irish lace sheers, making away with Momma's jewels. Not that they were much to start with: a couple of small, old-fashioned diamond rings, and the pearls Daddy had given Momma when they were first married, things like that. Earlene was welcome to them; I wouldn't wear that stuff on a dare, and Wayne would have ended up trading them for a magic bean or something.

Still, I sort of resented Miss Carlotta dining Earlene out, even if she was a widow and had lost Tiffany Crystal, her only child, and her life had been a series of tragic losses.

Then it occurred to me that Miss Carlotta had probably seen that professor guy going into the house last night, and God only knew what she would be telling Earlene about that, not to mention everyone else down to the Curl Up 'n' Dye.

Miss Carlotta writes the "Oysterback Social Notes" column for the *Bugeye,* our local paper. I guess Helga Wallop, the editor, figures that since Carlotta is the town gossip, she may as well get paid for it.

The fiddler crabs in the ditch waved their black claws at me as I walked past, as if they thought I could do something about the dry weather. I had to lift my feet to avoid stepping on them as they scuttled across the hot asphalt. A pair of claws, scuttling across the bottom of the road, like something from a poem by T. S. Eliot. Oh, Eliot would have loved Oysterback, I thought sourly, pleased with my own cleverness.

Omar Hinton's store has been down at the corner of Log Cabin Lane and Black Dog Road for as long as anyone can recall. His father had the place before he did. It's just far enough away that it's inconvenient to walk, but still close enough that you feel guilty if you hop in your car just to get a quart of milk and a bag of Happy Cat.

Hinton's is an old country store where all the retired watermen and farmers hang out, and there they were this morning, sitting around the cold woodstove on two long rows of wooden benches, enjoying the frigid blasts from the air conditioner mounted in the wall above their heads, all of them lazy, gossipy, and every bit as worn out as old sneakers. Faraday Hicks, Wilbur Rivers, and Ferrus T. Buckett were the regulars assembled there that morning. There used to be a few more of them, but they tended, at their age, to drop off the perch now and then, and no new generation of retirees had yet risen to take their empty seats.

But oh, can they tell tales, spinning stories that would have made Scheherazade envious, although looking at them this morning, playing dominoes, you'd never guess that they're such creative liars. They were all speculating on the new "film-at-eleven" story, namely the whereabouts of Alonzo Deaver. But now, with me showing up to provide fresh meat for the Audrey story, they perked up considerably.

I just sort of grunted at them as I went for the coffee pot, not really in the mood for the inevitable expressions of sympathy about my dead mother until I had some caffeine. The floorboards creaked beneath me, old pine planks worn smooth and silver from years of shuffling feet.

Omar was behind the counter, fanning himself with a copy of *TV Guide* as he restocked the bowed glass candy counter with Snickers and Reese's cups. The store was fragrant with fried scrapple and that old-man smell of laundry soap and pipe tobacco and motor oil. I helped myself to a Styrofoam cup and poured thick black coffee into it, then stirred in half-and-half until it was a nice, milky brown. No cheesy powdered creamer for Omar. He is a firm believer in the real. Real milk, real coffee, real sugar. When you do the bulk of your business with people who start work at five A.M., you have to understand that coffee is an art form. You should be able to stand up a spoon in it. A man who rises at four, travels a half hour by boat, at dawn, to spend his day running trotlines; a man who's out in the field at four, tilling his soybeans or tending to his chicken houses— such a man wants that first swallow of coffee to hit the back of his throat and stay there until the caffeine starts pumping through his bloodstream. You could use Omar's coffee to jump-start a dead battery.

"Oh, it's Carrie," Omar said by way of greeting when I went to pay for my coffee. He put down his paper and stroked the place on top of his head where his hair used to be. He studied me from behind his black Buddy Holly glasses. The funny thing about Omar is that he hasn't changed all that much since I was a kid and used to come in here for an ice-cream cone on hot summer nights. He's always looked the same, always been the same.

"Thelma and I were really shocked to hear about Audrey. It's a shock! I can't quite believe it yet! You have no idea what her loss will mean to this town." As mayor, of course he would think about the larger civic implications. He nodded mournfully. "You know, Audrey always seemed like the picture of health to me. She isn't—wasn't—more'n a year younger than me. It's going to be hard to think of things around here without her. Audrey was a take-charge kind of gal."

"Thanks," I said politely. "It was something of a shock to me too." I wasn't really listening to what was said because I really didn't want to talk about it all that much. Unspoken between us lay the silent accusation that I could have done better with my life and now my mother wouldn't be able to see me settle down and act like a normal Oysterback girl. I had long ago resigned myself to the idea that I was always going to be a kid to Omar, who is my mother's cousin.

"When's the funeral? Does Earlene have it scheduled yet?" Omar asked, counting out my change into my palm. I must have been short; he reached into the need-a-penny-take-a-penny-have-a-penny-leave-a-penny dish and helped the register to four cents.

I pulled a packet of Little Debbie Devil Cremes off the rack on the counter and opened the cellophane with my teeth. "It's a long story," I began. I knew Omar and the Liars' Bench would have the time to hear it; I just didn't feel like telling it. Besides, the way news travels around here, they probably knew more than I did and just wanted the official second source to back up the facts.

"Omar, why do you ask what *Earlene* has planned? Don't you think Wayne and I have any say? Delmar and Wayne will be coming back up with Momma's ashes, from Miami, and then we'll all see."

Omar grunted. "If you ask me, Wayne has already done more than his share to mess things up."

There was some muted agreement from the Liars' Bench, but when I turned to glare, everyone looked innocent.

"Well, you know what he's like. They're holding him in what I guess is the Miami airport jail 'til Delmar can get every-thing all straightened out, which should be happening right about now." I looked at the old Regulator clock on the wall above the door. Not that time means anything here—time is all these old guys have.

"Poor Wayne." Omar shook his head. "I heard tell he tried to carry Audrey's ashes in a metal urn onto the plane and it set off all the bells and whistles."

"You have the same story I do."

"Then we heard that this big ole security gal ast him to open the container, and he wouldn't let go," Wilbur Rivers said, although it came out as a question. "And they got him in some kind of mess down there and Delmar had to fly down last night to straighten it all out?"

"That's the story I heard."

"For someone who's supposed to be such a genius, Wayne can sure act sporty sometimes. What was he thinkin'? Things bein' what they are and all, I wouldn't be makin' no fuss at no

airport." Wilbur shook his head so vigorously, his Patamoke
Seafood cap bobbed all over his skimpy head.

"Listen to the world traveler!" Ferrus snorted. "Like you
ever been further than the Bay Bridge. How come you know so
much about airports?"

"Well, we have cable TV now. I watch the news, don't I?"
Wilbur asked.

"Well, Wayne was all upset, you can just bet." Ferrus
stretched out his legs. "After all, witnessin' his poor mother
fallin' into that pit of alligators and all couldn't have been easy,
especially for him, bein' you know, a genius and all."

"If Wayne's always been so goddamned much smarter than
everybody else, how come he's always gettin' inta trouble?"

"Because he's different. Them there genius fellas have their
minds somewhere else, thinkin' about science an' art an' deep
stuff like that."

"They don't think about regular stuff like you, who dropped
out in the eighth grade, Wilbur."

"I was bored."

"You was eighteen and they ast you to leave," someone corrected him. "You failed eighth grade four times in a row."

"So, I ain't no genius. That's for sure. But I'm smart enough
to know when not to mess with folks."

"Wayne's life hasn't been easy. First he went away to that
special genius school Audrey found for 'im when they figgered
out his Eye Que was off the charts, then he went to college
when he was like fourteen. Then he got hired by the gummit,
out there in Studio 54."

"Zone 51. And it was Los Alamos. You know, where they
make all them invisible stealth weapons and atomic bombs and
stuff."

"Well, I tell you, they must have done some kind of gummit
experiment on him, because he had that there nervous attack

and Audrey had to go out there and put 'im in that special hospital for real nervous smart people. Ever since he got fired from that there top secret gummit project, he's been wanderin' the country. Ever' once in a while, Audrey had to go straighten 'im out somewhere."

"I heard the gummit fired 'im because he had a nervous breakdown thing. Isn't that right, Carrie? That's what your momma said."

I was starting to crackle. I'd had to listen to people's ideas about Wayne ever since they found out his IQ was enormous. Even though I'd known these old guys all my life and was related by blood or marriage to nearly every one of them, even though I'd been brought up to respect my elders, I was about one step away from spraying some serious verbal insults around the room. After all, they were nearly all related to Wayne too. And if you asked me, every damn one of them was just as crazy as he ever was.

"Wayne was doing really well in Key West. He liked it there," Ferrus pointed out. "He found a job he liked, and people who liked him. But bein' a produce clerk in a supermarket wasn't good enough to suit Audrey. She had to go down there and prod him, just like she always did."

And you see what happened lay unspoken in the air. Somehow or other, everything that happens ends up being a moral tale to these people. And the moral is anyone who leaves town ends up badly.

"The funny thing is that Wayne and Alonzo were buddies back there when they were kids. Now, here they are, twenny years later, and both of them is in trouble again. Sometimes I don't think there's all that much difference between bein' really smart and bein' as dumb as cat shit."

"How would you know?" Ferrus asked sharply, and they all laughed. The talk turned back to Alonzo's escape.

As if he had read my thoughts and found them ungenerous, which they probably were, Omar quickly asked, "So, how long do you think you'll stay around this time? Still in the junk bidness? Still runnin' up and down the road?"

"Antiques. They're antiques," I replied automatically. If I had gone to Hollywood and won an Oscar and made a million dollars, people around here probably would have asked if I was still trying to get into acting. If it doesn't actually happen right there in Oysterback, it doesn't really happen. I swallowed and forced myself to smile. "I guess I'll stay 'til the funeral, then I'll get back to work. I'm still in business, and still runnin' the roads." I tested a smile, but it didn't quite work.

"Thought maybe by now, you'd be thinking about settling down again," Omar offered. "Now that your mother's gone and everything. Someone's gonna have to live in that house. House no one lives in goes to pot fast."

"Well, I guess Earlene can put one of her sons in it," I replied vaguely. "She'd probably be thrilled if they moved out of her place. They're certainly old enough to."

Omar looked at me over his glasses again. "Well, be that as it may, Carrie, but what you do's not what I would want for one of my daughters. Or my sons, either," he added almost as an afterthought.

Here we go again, I thought. To Omar, and probably everyone else around here, there's something wrong—maybe even whorish—about a woman who travels, who does what I do, buying and selling stuff. "I'm an antique dealer, not a truck-stop trollop, Omar. I don't know why you people don't know the difference—"

Omar threw his hands up, palms out. "Come on, now, Carrie. I've known you since you were born! No need to get hinky on me! You're a grown woman! It's just that, well, you *are* a grown woman, that's all."

Well, I couldn't fight with Omar. He's family, and besides, he means well. So I mumbled an apology. "This whole thing has me all upset," I said, knowing I sounded churlish, even to myself. But people are more likely to excuse you on account of death. Look at the bad behavior Miss Carlotta's gotten away with for years and years on account of being a widow who lost her promising daughter. Surely I was entitled to a little bit of slack myself.

Omar didn't look as if he were going to cut me any, though, so I changed the subject. "What about Alonzo Deaver escaping from jail?" I tried.

Well, people die all the time, but someone escaping from jail is a novelty. Omar perked right up. "They said on the news he was spotted in Crofton, last night, using a pay phone," he informed me.

"He'll be comin' back here, just you wait and see," Faraday Hicks volunteered from the Liars' Bench. The only sound you could hear from that crowd might be the click of the domino tiles, but you can bet they never miss a word.

"That's right, Alonzo'll be back. He's an Eastern Shore boy. He's headin' across the bridge, you wait and see."

"Comin' back to Oysterback, thass what Alonzo's gonna do, just like his daddy used to do when they carried 'im over to jail that time. Them Deavers is all alike."

"Well, sir, I tell ya, it'll give that there college professor, that Jack, something more to write about than the good old days, I tell you that. We haven't had this much excitement around town since Johnny Ray run the cruiser into the side of the post office, lookin' for those Iranians the boys told him about."

"I thought they was Uranians, from the planet Uranus." They all chuckled at their joke, and I just knew they'd told Jack Shepherd that tale a time or two. The deputy sheriff's incompetence was legendary.

I took my coffee and my Little Debbie Devil Creme and went and sat on the edge of one of the two benches, just far enough away from the old guys as not to threaten them, but close enough to be sociable. It seemed like an adequate revenge for them making fun of my brother Wayne.

They stirred like a broody house of old hens when they smell a hawk, ripples of stirred feathers. I would now be willing to bet good money that they had been talking about Momma until I came in. Probably not saying much that was good, either. At one time or another, Momma had flirted with all of them, I was sure. She could no more be around a man and not flirt than most people could quit breathing. Nonetheless, my female presence among them had them riled up, but that was different, because I was meeting them as if I were a member of the club. It was just the cherry on top of the guilt they felt for dissing the deceased.

Plus, these old guys come down to the store to get away from the women, not to have one settle herself among them, but I'm an old hand at ruffling feathers, and so I just sat patiently, sipping at my coffee and chewing my Devil Creme. I avoided eye contact, sneaking looks around Omar's store to see if there was anything, however insignificant, that I could acquire for stock. When you don't throw anything out, ever, some of it actually becomes quite collectible. Old tools, patent medicines, advertising stuff—you name it. It may look like junk to you, but there's someone out there that will pay top dollar for it, believe me. Was that a six-pack of Billy Beer behind those fan belts? I was a hawk all right, but these men weren't my prey. Stuff was.

Wilbur Rivers started telling me how sorry he was about Momma by recounting a long and pointless story about how he had cut up a dead tree in her backyard and hauled it away after Hurricane Camille. I pretended to listen as I scanned the dusty shelves in the back of the store where the Redball boots and camouflage jumpsuits were displayed, next to the videotapes and cereal boxes. I thought I saw a fifties-era placard for Blue Star Headache Powders propping up a display for Bud Lite. A hundred bucks, easy.

"It took me three trips to get rid of all the wood from that tree," Wilbur was recalling happily. "I'd fill up the truck, drive it out to the dump, let 'er off, go back, and fill 'er up again. That was some big ole tree, lemme tell ya. I had to get Fred Hogarth over there to help me."

As he nattered on, I studied the Liars' Bench. Old retired men with faces cracked and worn like old leather from a lifetime on the water, in the field. Hands like red cedar roots, twisted from arthritis and hard work. A couple of them had lost their teeth and never bothered to replace them; they grew up in a time when dental hygiene was unknown. Three old guys who wore their pants up around their armpits and shirts closed tight at the collar with bolo ties. Guys who suddenly find themselves with vast, hanging gardens of time on their hands, suspended between work and the time until they, too, die.

You can mow the lawn only so often; the paper takes only so much time to read. Their wives, having kept house perfectly well for fifty years, do not take kindly to be followed around by a retired husband telling them how to cook and clean, or suggesting a better way to make a bed. So the old guys migrate to Omar's store to sit on the benches, play dominoes, and hang out with their peer group. And the herd thins out a little more every year; cancer and Florida and a lifetime of hard work and being just plain worn out catches up with them. So they spend a few hours with spades and dominoes, clinging to the familiar, growing suspicious and reactionary; anything new must be a bad thing to these guys. For them, the last great unknown is death, and they can wait on that.

You know that Igmar Bergman movie where this knight

comes home from some crusade or something and ends up playing chess with Death? I saw that one in college. Well, if Death came into Omar Hinton's store, he could sit right down on a bench and start playing dominoes with Faraday Hicks and Ferrus T. Buckett. If Death wore his pants up under his armpits, told creative lies, and treated them all to a Mountain Dew, he'd fit right in. In fact, he'd be so comfortable, he'd probably never leave, and if that had happened, then maybe Momma wouldn't be in a metal container at the Miami airport.

Yes, and maybe pigs would fly. Again, I felt the unexpected sting of tears as loss hit me once more. I must have shown it, too, for Wilbur trailed off, patting me uncertainly on the shoulder with a shaky old hand. These men really didn't mean any harm. Talk was about all they had left in them.

"Ya, sorry about Audrey. She was something else," Faraday Hicks rumbled. "I guess you just never know. Lookit me. Remember when they sent me up to Hopkins? They opened me up and saw that I was full of cancer, so they sewed me back up and sent me home to die. Said I had six months." He grinned, showing me a neat row of dentures.

Ferrus chuckled and continued the story. "That were six years ago! He gave the farm over to his son and lay down on the couch, waitin' to die."

"Everyone in town come by to say their last good-byes," Wilbur observed. "He even got himself saved by Reverend Claude Crouch, just in case."

"We thought the next time we'd see him, he'd be in a box over to Dreedle's Funeral Home."

"Well, I lay up on the sofa for a couple of months. Started up watchin' soap operas." He deftly reached into the box and pulled out a domino, looked at it, and sighed regretfully as he placed it on the table. "I was getting so depressed watchin' that stuff, I started to hope that I would die. Them stories is just awful—people sleepin' with each every other and havin' babies and getting' themselves into the worst damn predicaments—but they get you hooked and you have to watch." Wilbur selected a domino, and with a snort of triumph, matched it to one on the table. He grinned at Faraday, who just shook his head.

"Finally, one day Audrey come over and she says, 'Faraday, you've laid up on that couch for well on to a year now. It's just about time you decided you're gonna live and get on up off there and be about your business.'"

"That sounds like Momma," I agreed.

"She ripped that afghan right offen me," Faraday recalled complacently. "Made me get up on outta there and run the bush hog through the greenbrier down by the creek. A week later, I was still workin', and it's been over six years. That doctor up to Hopkins who told me I onny had six months keeled over dead on his sailboat two years ago. And I'm still goin' on." He gave a deep phlegmy cough of satisfaction.

"Onny trouble is, I'd already signed the farm over to my son. And he wasn't givin' it back! Why should he? He'd been waitin' for me to retire for ten years! He's got three kids to educate! So, I ask you, what the hell am I supposed to do with myself?"

I crumbled up my Devil Creme wrapper. "The opportunities for volunteer work are endless," I replied as I slowly got up and tossed the wrapper into the cold stove. "Think of the future old guys y'all could be trainin' to take your places on these benches."

I heard Wilbur chuckling as I walked away. The Blue Star placard could wait for a couple of days. I didn't want to look too eager, or Omar would want an arm and a leg for it. We go through this every time I come home, and he generally tries to get the best of me. Sometimes he wins, sometimes I do. It's all a game.

But I was no sooner out the door when I heard Ferrus coming up behind me.

Now, of all the old retired watermen and farmers, Ferrus T. Buckett is about the oldest. He's somewhere between eighty and death. Some guy once came down here from the *Sun* and wrote this whole article about how Ferrus was so elderly and still working the water. He's never been married, and he lives down at the end of Black Dog Road in this falling-down house that he shares with his dog, Boston Blackie, who is, of course, a black Lab, and every bit as old as Ferrus.

"What have you got for me?" I asked him as soon as we walked over behind his ancient pickup. I leaned against the sideboard and watched as he fumbled purposefully around among the crab baskets and burlap sacks.

With a flourish, he withdrew a wooden carving. It was an ancient duck decoy, an oldsquaw drake, black and white, looking as if it was in its original paint. I don't know a whole lot about old decoys, but I know there's a huge market for certain long-dead carvers. The deader, the better, as most of the people who collect decoys would not have cared to associate with the illiterate, unwashed scofflaws who carved them. Oh, no.

"That's a really nice one," I said admiringly, turning it over in my hands. It had a balanced, graceful shape. The keel was weighted down with a piece of lead, which gave it a comforting heft. It would ride gracefully in the water, should anyone care to hunt over it, which I doubted they would. "It looks like an Ira Hudson."

Ferrus coughed modestly but said nothing. It was up to me to make an offer or to decline.

"Uh, how's twenty-five suit you?" I tried.

Ferrus stared off across the soybean fields. His blue eyes didn't blink.

"Thirty?"

No response.

"Forty?"

Ferrus cleared his throat of a rich coat of phlegm.

"Okay! Okay! Fifty!"

A grin flickered across his face.

I pulled out my wad, admittedly a thin one, and counted out five tens into his hand. He stuffed them into his shirt pocket. "I've got a couple of geese out to the house if you're interested. They're just about ripe enough to dig out of the manure pile."

I grinned. "I'll stop by." I held the duck carefully in my hands. It was a real work of art, beautifully painted, not too slick and not too crude. "Ferrus," I asked again, "why do you forge these birds? You could make a wonderful living if you sold your decoys under your own name, a guy like you, old outlaw gunner and all. You could set up at any decoy show anywhere and win yourself a ton of attention and money. You could be famous."

Ferrus winked. "What would be the fun in that?" he asked with a grin, ever the old outlaw.

Then he totally surprised me. He leaned over and looked at me hard out of those faded blue eyes, the color of a winter river. "Don't be so hard to judge your mother or Earlene," he said. "You don't know everything you think you do, Carrie. You've got a hell of a lot to find out, my girl."

I wanted to get mad, but I couldn't. What did this old man think he knew that I didn't? He didn't grow up with those two. And I was about to say as much when I took another look at him and knew that he was telling me the truth.

"What do I need to know?" I asked uncertainly.

Ferrus shook his head. "The whole story's out there, waiting to be told. Just hang around long enough and you'll find out," he said. I watched him as he walked over to the cab, climbed in, started the engine, and put his truck in gear. "Rain comin' tonight," he said, and rolled away, leaving me to stare at his fender through a cloud of dust.

It's generally accepted around these parts that Ferrus knows things, sees things that are going to happen. I don't believe in that stuff myself, but sometimes I have to wonder.

6

Whole Lotta Shakin'
Goin' On

Ferrus was probably right: the whole story was just out there, ready to be told, but I didn't know what it was—yet.

His prediction about rain that night was surely dead wrong, though. The sky was huge and cloudless, and the sun was high now, bright and hot. Not so much as a breath of air stirred the dust, and the humidity just clung to everything, and it wasn't going anywhere anytime soon.

Across the street and down the block a bit, just before you get to the Curl Up 'n' Dye, and right after you pass the post office going toward Tubman's Corners, the Blue Crab Tavern sits in all its glory.

Here, Desiree holds court and will have you know that she owns three stars for the quality of her cuisine. I know a lot of people are stunned to find a three-star restaurant in a two-bit town out on the marsh, but that's the way it is. The Elvis mural on the side of the Bahama pink building—the side that faces the softball field—just hints at what's inside.

It takes a while to adjust to the low light, but when you do, the first thing your eye falls on is the Elvis shrine over the back bar. There's a huge picture of Elvis on black velvet, surrounded by twinkling lights and all sorts of Elvis-themed stuff. Since the man died, I don't think there's a cheap plastic surface that his image can't be placed on, so you can just imagine. I don't know if Desiree set out to decorate the Blue Crab in Elvisness, but at some point, people started bringing her stuff with a King theme, and it just grew. Now she accepts every offered item and adds it to the vast and spreading collage that is slowly taking over the place. Kind of like Elvis kudzu.

Right before she came back here for good, after her next-to-last husband, Milo Mildeaux, died, Desiree went on a spiritual quest to Tibet, in search of what she calls the True Meaning of Life. "I was meditating with the Bah' Lama," she told me years later, "and all of a sudden I had this vision of Elvis. He was on this gold cloud, wearing this white suit and smiling. He said, 'Whole lotta shakin' goin' on.' Just that. Nothing else. The Bah' Lama said, 'Well, that's your vision. Obviously, Elvis is your spirit guide. Note that of all his lifetime incarnations—young Elvis, rebel Elvis, movie Elvis—he chose to appear to you as Vegas Elvis.' I'd never even thought about Elvis before that. I mean, he was our parents' generation, but I decided, well, what the hell, I can walk in Elvisness as well as anything else, and from that moment on, I've never had any more problems with spiritual enlightenment."

And as far as I know, she hasn't.

When I walked in, she was up behind the bar, chalking up the lunch menu on the blackboard. Today the Blue Crab was featuring Thai lemongrass soup and grilled chicken with peanut sauce. I could smell the soup, rich and pungent, as I walked in.

In a town where the most exotic seasoning is Old Bay, Desiree's cooking was looked upon suspiciously at first, as if she were practicing witchcraft with star anise and mace. But now everybody comes here to eat, even if they would never cook things like that at home, dishes such as her white meat loaf and garlic mashed potatoes.

"Hi, Carrie!" She jumped down. "How are you feeling?"

"Like I was hit by a truck," I replied, which was churlish but true.

Desiree's mass of bloodred hair bobbed. "Yeah, that's how it feels," she said matter-of-factly. "Every single time. Losing a parent is tough. It's not easy being an orphan, no matter how old you are." She thrust her head through the hatchway between the bar and the kitchen. "Beth," she called to her help, "when you get a chance, set the rice steamer on, okay?"

Beth, an uncertain young woman whose existence seemed to revolve around the complex ongoing drama of her social life and her turbulent marriage to Paisley Redmond, sighed loudly.

"What is it now?" I asked, sotto voce.

Desiree rolled her eyes. "What is it always? He said, she said, they fight, they make up, they fuck. Right now, they're fighting because she says he looked at some girl in the Buy 'n' Bag in town yesterday. God, I'm so glad I'm not twenty anymore."

I nodded in complete agreement. "I'm also glad I'm single and childless," I added with a great sense of self-satisfaction, which I really needed to feel right then.

Desiree pulled some napkins from beneath the counter, sat down, and started folding them. I picked up a handful and followed her lead, just to have something to do with my hands.

"You know, it's okay to cry," she said. "And it's okay to feel bad, and to want to talk about Audrey. And every once in a while, when you least expect it, you'll find yourself crying for no reason. It happens for months afterward."

"I'm okay," I said shortly. "Really. I am."

Desiree threw me a sharp look. I could sense her thinking, *Yeah, right,* but she didn't say it out loud. She didn't need to.

"You know, most people are really uncomfortable around a grieving person. Ask Parsons Dreedle sometime. With the funeral home and all, he sees it all the time."

"Oh, my Lord, I bet Earlene never even thought to call Parsons, what with Wayne cremating Momma down there and everything. He'll be so hurt, you know. He was really looking forward to burying Momma, just like he buried Daddy."

"Well, you can let him open the grave and make all the arrangements for the memorial service," she said. "That should make him happy."

"I guess I'll have to talk to Earlene about it. God," I whined, "I don't want to talk to Earlene about anything, but especially not this. Miss Carlotta told me that she's been takin' boxes and boxes of stuff out of Momma's house already."

"Well, that's Earlene. Or not. I don't know if you or Miss Carlotta should jump to conclusions. You don't know what's in those boxes."

I thought that over for a moment. "Well, I guess she could be hauling home baked goods and casseroles. I never saw so much food in my life, and we can't possibly eat it all, not even with Audrey's little friend crashing on the daybed."

"Hey, Carrie! I won't eat much," Jack Shepherd called. "Freeze all that stuff. You'll need it for the wake."

To my utter horror, I realized that he had been washing glasses down at the other end of the bar the whole time. I'd forgotten that he worked here. And now he'd overheard my girlish conversation with Desiree. Great. I had no privacy in this town.

Desiree's fingers moved swiftly, folding napkins in half, stacking them on the counter. She glanced at the plastic Elvis clock on the wall, his legs swinging back and forth like a pendulum, as if he were swiveling his hips. Cute. "Want to have some lunch before the rush hits?"

"No, thanks. I couldn't shove a bite of food in my mouth," I muttered. "Not with my foot in there."

Desiree's eyes slid in Jack's direction, but he was already doing setups on the tables.

"Who *is* he?" I whispered. "What his story?"

Before she could reply, the doors banged open and a couple of watermen shuffled in, dragging their heavy rubber boots across the floor. The rush had started.

The men smelled of the outdoors, of salt water and sunshine, fuel and fish, and they were laughing.

"Oh, my Gawd," the taller one boomed. "I seen that van around town and I said to myself, is Carrie come visiting us?" He grinned at me, punching his friend in the upper arm. Junior Redmond's smile creased his whole good-natured open face.

"Hi, Carrie, sorry about your mother," his companion muttered. Hudson Swann didn't quite look at me as he shuffled down the bar and took a seat, studying the menu with great interest. And in case you are wondering, yes, Hudson is my distant cousin. So is Junie. In Oysterback, the kinship ties are complex, reaching back over hundreds of years. Someone like Jack Shepherd probably needed to be told to be careful what he said about people before he knew who was connected to whom and why. Or maybe he'd already figured that out.

"Oh, damn, Carrie, I forgot." Junior, remembering himself, wiped the smile off his face. "We were really sorry to hear about Miss Audrey," he said uncomfortably.

"It just doesn't seem real somehow, Miss Audrey bein' gone like that," Hudson observed. "But I'm real sorry, and so is Jeanne. You know, she did Miss Audrey's hair every single week. I think she's kind of disappointed that she won't be able to do her for the funeral, Miss Audrey being cremated and all."

I couldn't imagine Jeanne Swann being disappointed not to

have to go over to Dreedle's Funeral Home to wash and set the hair on a corpse. But I guess when you work at the Curl Up 'n' Dye, and so many of your clients around here are waiting for the Great Hairdresser in the Sky, you get to do the hair of quite a few of the formerly living.

"Doreen and I are real sorry," Junior added, patting my hand.

He stood there for a moment, shifting from side to side, smiling at me and nodding, and I realized that he was hideously uncomfortable in the presence of death, and couldn't wait to get away from me, lest it be contagious.

Hudson, on the other hand, had always been very good at ignoring unpleasantness.

"You setting out pots yet?" I asked, hoping a change of subject would ease the discomfort somewhat.

You could almost see both men relax, see the tension draining from the pair of them, shifting off their spines and down into their boots. When you mentioned a safe subject like crabbing, they knew where they stood. They could talk about crabbing all day. Still, I think they were relieved when Desiree asked if they wanted their usual and they were able to sit down at the other end of the bar and eat cheeseburgers and not think about death anymore.

Just then, the door banged open and eight or nine guys started to file in, in ones and twos, coming in off the water. The first one looked like a professional wrestler who had spent a bad night in the county detention center, and they went downhill from there.

The TV over the bar was turned on, and *The Guiding Light*'s syrupy theme overtook Elvis on the jukebox. As one, the guys all turned to look at the screen, and Desiree started to hustle cheeseburgers and chicken satay.

For the next hour, no one spoke above a whisper. Those great big hairy men sat there with their chicken half chewed as they stared at the TV screen, their rapt attention held by the improbable story of misdeeds, affairs, and buff bodies. I guess if you knew what was going on, it was interesting, but I didn't have the faintest. If I could have gotten over my own inertia, I would have been on my merry way, but Desiree slipped me a cup of lemongrass soup, and it went down slow and easy on top of my Little Debbie breakfast.

"I'm Reva Shane, and don't you forget it!" one of the Guiding Light actresses announced as she burst into a room. She was clearly plenty pissed off.

"Who the hell is Reva Shane?" Jack Shepherd whispered to me as he offloaded luncheon specials down the bar. "And why would anyone forget it?"

"Quiet!" the burly guy next to me said, never taking his eyes from the screen. "Reva's about to tear Tory a new one!"

"*The Guiding Light* is the preferred soap opera of watermen everywhere," I whispered. "It comes on just as they're getting in off the water. Otherwise, they'd all be watching *The Young and the Restless.*"

The notebook and pen came out. Jack looked at me expectantly. I shrugged. "It's just one of those things. Haven't you noticed that when they're all out on the water, they talk on the radio about what happened on the *Light* the day before?"

"Why do you think they like this particular soap?"

"Why don't you ask them? Because I have no idea, except it's been on as long as anyone can remember, and their fathers probably watched it, too."

"Watch it, Reva! Josh has a gun!" someone down the bar yelled.

"Where were you yesterday, Bunk? That's not Josh, that's Josh's evil twin!" Jack exclaimed, then gave me a sheepish grin.

"Ask them. Just don't ask them while they're watching," I whispered.

"Sure."

"Quiet down! The evil Josh is about to confront the real Josh!"

"Well, what did you expect? He's been planning this for weeks," Jack said, turning his attention to the screen again.

"Well, that's the whole point," someone explained. "Whoa! Watch it, Evil Josh! Here come Reva!"

I watched as the professor scribbled something in his notebook. "Can we talk about this later when I get off?" he whispered without looking at me. The TV just had them all fixated. I could have exploded a bomb in there and no one would have noticed.

Having had all the drama I thought I could handle, I paid for my lunch and ambled outside.

The day had turned sullen. The light was white-hot, bleaching the landscape. A thick, viscous humidity had settled in for the afternoon, and the sun beat mercilessly down on the marsh and the open fields. Coming out of the air-conditioning, I gasped.

With most of my day so far shot in trips down memory lane, I figured I'd given Earlene plenty of time to get in and out of the house with whatever booty she wanted. It was too late now to even think about conducting any business.

I started to walk home, cutting across the Blue Crab's softball field and into the shade at the edge of the woods, along the path I had followed as a kid, coming home from elementary school. Except there wasn't a school there anymore, just an old empty building that had been for sale for many years. Now the kids rode the bus to a big new consolidated school in town.

The tide was way out, leaving the air stained with the rough green scent of marsh. I sniffed, smiling in spite of an odor that frequently left outsiders gasping for air. Lost in memories of my misspent youth, I followed the path along the old ditch that was full of cattails and choked with phragmites. It wasn't until I saw the blue and white pickup parked around the side of the school that I realized someone knew exactly what I was doing and could predict where I'd go.

He was parked around the side, where no one could see him from the road. I found him leaning against the truck, watching the path as if he knew that sooner or later I would appear, trailing along like the last of the Mohicans.

He was just as handsome as ever, and his eyes were still green as the river. And when he grinned at me, that sheepish grin, I felt the old, familiar, and unwanted weakness in my knees and other places. I could barely stand to see him there, rocking back and forth on the soles of his feet in those tight jeans, but there he was, a ghost from my past.

"How ya really doin'?" Hudson Swann asked me, grinning all over himself.

"As well as could be expected," I replied, stopping to lean against the side of his truck. The metal was hot from the sun. "It's been a few years, hasn't it." I pulled the top of my shirt away from my neck. It was sticky with sweat.

"It's been a few years," he replied, moving to stand next to me. We both stared down into the flatbed of the truck, as if some old bushel baskets and a couple of coils of rope were the most fascinating things in the world.

"That long?" I asked, although I knew exactly how long it had been. "You look good. Marriage seems to agree with you."

"Jeanne's young," he said shortly, tracing a scratch in the panel with his finger, looking at me from beneath the bill of his cap.

"And very pretty," I added. "She was about five or six classes behind us, I think."

"More like ten or twelve."

"*Tiens!*" I murmured, knowing damn well he couldn't speak

French. Hell, he could barely speak English, for all of those two years of community college. And that time wasted, because here he was, working the water, still living in Oysterback, scraping by as a man of few words, and most of those referred to moving engine parts.

"I'm sorry about Miss Audrey," he said at last. "That was quite a shock, her dyin' down in Florida like that."

"She was always fond of you." I sounded prim, even to my own ears. When we'd broken up, Momma had a fit. She was afraid I'd never get a chance at marriage again, and I guess she was right. I studied a hard-shelled bug that was crawling along the scraped bottom of the flatbed. It disappeared beneath a rusted-out tong-head, and I waited for it to emerge on the other side.

"Kids?"

Then I had to look at him. "Me? Kids? Good Lord, no!" I exclaimed, shocked at the very thought. "No kids, no husband. Just the . . . business. Keeps me on the road a lot. You?"

"Two. Twin girls."

"Ah." Well, what else could I say?

"Ashley and Amber. They're five. Start kindergarten this fall."

"Ah." Ashley and Amber, I thought. Jeanne must have picked those names from some Aaron Spelling glitz fest. Figures. But I didn't say anything, just stared into the bottom of the truck, leaning against the hot fender, intensely aware of this man standing next to me. He smelled pleasantly of sunshine and salt water, and he was still a good-looking man.

"I think about you," Hudson finally said. He knotted his hands together, leaning on his elbows, looking at me out of the corner of his eyes. "A lot."

I squinted at him, his profile bleached by the hard light. "You have a funny way of showing it. You all but ignored me back at the Blue Crab."

"I'm a married man. People talk."

"But that was such a long time ago."

"Wasn't that long. We had something, you and me."

"Yeah, we had something. But we were young and dumb." And you married someone else, I thought.

"Maybe young, not dumb."

I really wasn't expecting what happened next, the way he gathered me up in his arms, and I certainly wasn't expecting that I would respond the way I did, going sort of limp. I thought I was long past the point when he could do those things to me, but I was wrong, wrong, *wrong*. And I wasn't expecting to be kissed, but I was. It shocked me; I was paralyzed by surprise, and not sure what to think about it.

"I did miss you," he said, his mouth against my ear. Just the soap and sunshine smell of him was almost enough to make me crazy right then and there. "No one can see us, here," he whispered.

I really wanted to let myself so, right there, in the back of his pickup. Well, some part of me wanted to. I'd never felt so lonely in my life, and even half a waterman was better than being alone with this hungry grief.

Then he took his hat off.

The mullet spilled down his back in a wavy stream of hair.

I could feel the romance bubble pop.

A mullet. A beavertail. A 7. One of the ugliest haircuts known to Western civilization. The Wal-Mart of hairstyles. You know, short in front and long in the back. The ultimate form of birth control, as far as I'm concerned. Yuck. Double yuck. Instant turn-off.

"I'm here because of my mother, not because of you," I finally said.

He let go of me then. Isn't it amazing what bringing up the subject of death can do to the male libido? Almost as much of a deflator as a mullet.

"I can wait," he announced.

I felt a hot flush creeping into my cheeks. Great, just what I needed. An old boyfriend with a yen to relive the past. An old *married* boyfriend with all the sensitivity you could expect from an old boyfriend. An old boyfriend who had grown . . . a mullet. "Besides," I added, "that was then, this is now."

"You're not gonna bring all that up again, are you?" He looked at me sullenly from beneath his eyelashes.

"I won't if you won't." I pushed myself away, turning to go.

"Carrie?"

I glanced back over my shoulder and wondered if I was making a mistake. He still had that effect on me, but then I saw the hair again, cascading down the back of his neck, waving in the breeze.

"I'm not goin' anywhere." He held my gaze for a second, then turned away.

Well, damn, I thought. What the hell was that all about?

Besides being a definite ego boost. It's always nice to know you still have it, even though you're not entirely certain what *it* is.

It's also a nice way of reminding myself why I am gun-shy about men, romance, and the whole damn sex thing.

Especially when men grow a mullet. Ick.

7

Funeral Meat, a Dish Best Tasted Cold

I was pondering the mysteries of why good hair goes bad as I turned and walked slowly down the road toward home. A small breeze had begun to stir off the river, no more than a baby's breath, but it sure felt good against my skin. It was hot enough to cook on the asphalt, some of which was now sticking to the soles of my sandals.

I was so involved in life on Planet Carrie that I barely noticed the traffic jam up ahead, in the middle of the two-lane blacktop. Hudson's pickup was parked neck and neck with a ratty old Volvo wagon.

Whoever Hudson was talking to, the conversation looked casual. He was laughing, until he caught sight of me walking down the shoulder. Then he said something to the person in the Volvo.

Jack Shepherd leaned out of the wagon, and the two of them grinned at me.

I had the uneasy feeling, studying them, that Jack might have seen that whole drama behind the old school. I wondered if *that* was going into his little notebook too.

The pair of them regarded me just long enough to make me

feel uneasy. Did I have something hanging out of my nose? Or worse, were they talking about me? I couldn't help but notice that this professor fellow seemed very cozy with the locals, which struck me as probably not being a good sign.

"I'll catch ya tonight!" Hudson concluded. My old boyfriend cast me a sour little smile as he took off down the road, and then I knew for sure I had been the subject of some, if not all, of their conversation. I guess I should have been flattered. Suspiciously, I drew abreast of the Volvo.

"Hey. I just got off work and I wondered if you could use a ride back down the road. It's awfully hot to be walking," Jack said enticingly.

If it had been less like breathing hot Jell-O out there, I would have been proud and paranoid enough to turn him down. But since it wasn't, I didn't, and so I waited for him to move all the papers and notebooks and stuff off the passenger seat so I could hop in.

"Sorry about that," he mumbled, tossing things into the backseat. "This is my traveling office, now that I don't have one up at the college."

"Yeah, I heard you didn't get tenure." The plastic seat was hot against my bare legs. No air-conditioning here, just little bits of paper and a forgotten marker pen that stuck to my sweaty thigh.

"Boy, you have no secrets around here, do you," he said cheerfully, like a man who, maddeningly, has nothing to hide.

"Hell, no. But as a student of small-town life, you should know that. Unless you're masquerading as a writer about small-town life and you're really something else." Oh, my paranoia was working overtime.

He laughed, a nice, self-deprecating laugh. "I wish I were something other than a failed academic."

I could have pursued that, but I decided it was better off left alone. Anyway, about that time we were turning into the driveway and parking behind the van.

"Mind if I come in for a minute? I need to pick up some stuff."

In spite of the high privet hedge, I could feel eyes tuned in on us behind every lace curtain on the road. "Watch yourself," I told Jack. "What Momma used to call the Neighborhood Watch is in full force, observing the goings-on at the Hudson house."

"You know, I thought I might have seen a venetian blind twitching occasionally on the street." Jack smiled, amused.

"Of course, they've been doing this for years. Momma's real-life dramas were better than anything on television, at least before they ran cable down this way," I told him. "I guess that's what happens when you live on a street full of elderly folks with too much time on their hands. And the old guys are just as bad as the women." I unlocked my van and scrambled around inside for my laptop.

In Miss Carlotta's dining room windows, a curtain quivered and fell back into place. To my utter surprise, the window sash rose and the lady herself, beaming all over, leaned out. "Yoo-hoo! Hello, Jack!" she called.

"How are you doing, Mrs. Hackett?" he responded easily. "Your headaches any better since you went to the doctor?"

"Don't get me started," she said with a big sigh. "But you're so sweet to ask."

I almost fell over. For Miss Carlotta to forgo giving a full recital of all her aches and pains was unheard of.

"I found those old photographs, the ones I told you about, the ones of my father making scrapple out on the farm!" She was just shining all over him, sounding like Glinda the Good Witch.

"They really brought back some memories of the old days when everyone around here kept a hog or two."

"Good! I'll be anxious to take a look at them! Remember, you said you were going to sit down and let me get your memories of your father's market gunning."

"Oh, I haven't forgotten!" Good Lord, she was positively flirtatious. She was actually smiling at him.

"Maybe if you're not busy later . . ." Jack called over the hedge. He tapped the notebook in his shirt pocket.

"That would be fine. Come by any time!" She was absolutely trilling as she waved at him and closed the window, trapping the frosty air inside her closed-up, air-conditioned home. I bet that was the first time she'd opened a window in years.

"Well, look at you," I said, coming up with my laptop and clutching it to my chest. "I didn't think it was possible, but somehow or another, you charmed the old girl."

Jack shrugged. "She's a perfectly nice old lady. And she has some great memories of growing up on a farm out near Tubman's Corners."

I guess charming Miss Carlotta was a part of his job, but I'd never seen her act so civil to a stranger before. She'd never even acted nice to me like that, and I'd known her all my life.

Jack held the screen door for me. It was slightly cooler inside the house, and several new funeral dishes had made an appearance since midmorning. I gazed in dismay at a Pyrex casserole of corn pudding, a Saran-Wrapped Bundt cake, and some baked macaroni and cheese all placed neatly on the kitchen table where you couldn't miss them.

"I don't know where we're going to find room for all this stuff," I sighed. "The freezer is full already because Mama never threw anything out . . ."

Jack selected a cookie from a plate on the countertop. "It

looks like a bake sale in here." He talked with his mouth full, little bits of crumb spilling down the front of his shirt. "Mmmm. Good. Tell ya what. If you've got a basket or a box or something, I'll take some of this stuff over and ask Mrs. Hackett if I can put it in her refrigerator. She doesn't have much in there, living alone."

I had to stare. That Jack Shepherd, a stranger, knew what Miss Carlotta kept in her refrigerator was beyond comprehension. I don't think even Momma had that sort of information. Miss Carlotta was private, to say the least.

"I sort of doubt she'd help us out," I managed to say. "She keeps her house hermetically sealed, so the dirt from this place doesn't blow in her windows. She's always looked down on Momma's housekeeping . . ."

Bad housekeeping just being one of many other things Miss Carlotta didn't like about us. Including, one might have thought, Professor Shepherd himself, since he seemed to be quite at home chez Audrey.

As I plugged in the laptop and connected to my ISP, I wondered what his secret was with older women. And ex-boyfriends. And, it sounded like, just about everyone else in this one-horse town. While I, a native and a local, couldn't get arrested by my own people for awfulness, Jack Shepherd blew in here and became One of Us.

Grimacing, I logged on to eBay and punched in my password. My little laptop hummed and strummed, connecting across the miles.

"Nice computer. I notice you're a Mac person. Me, I'm PC," Jack mused as he poked through the broom closet.

"There's a major religious difference between us right there," I muttered, scanning a few items I was bidding on. So far, I was losing out on a Flexible Flyer sled in medium condition and winning a collection of plastic Halloween toys from the sixties by bidding slightly more than I had planned. Halloween is a hot niche market.

"You might want to reconsider that *Petticoat Junction* lunch box. It should be Ginger and Mary Ann, not Billie Jo and Bobbie Jo. Now, Elly Mae Clampett, she was hot." I glared at him and he stopped looking over my shoulder.

I upped the bid on the lunch box just to show him, even though it was already bidding way above resale value.

Jack had found a cardboard flat and was busy gathering up stray funeral goodies. "Mrs. Hackett's a sweet old lady," he informed me as he went out the door. "You just don't know how to handle older women."

"And I notice that you do," I snapped. Honestly, had the man no shame? Momma's ashes weren't even back from Florida and he was already all over Miss Carlotta. But if he expected to get lucky there, he could just forget it. I don't think she'd done the nasty since Mr. Hackett met an untimely end more than thirty years ago, running his Monte Carlo head-on into a Chinaberry Farms Poultry truck on Route 50.

I was still staring at the computer screen, my mind a million miles away from a *Hart to Hart* board game (Mint Condition, We Accept Pay Pal), when Earlene kicked open the screen door, her arms full of floral arrangements. "These will wilt in this heat before the funeral," she said by way of greeting.

"At least it's not more food," I replied without taking my eyes off the screen.

"Is that one of those Internet things? You have to be careful with that, I hear tell it's all full of pornography and people trying to get your credit card number." She set the arrangements in the sink, peering over my shoulder nonetheless. She'd just gotten off work and she smelled of fried food, onions, and fatigue.

"Join the twenty-first century, Earlene. You could learn a lot if you were willing to get e-mail and check things on the Web. At least Wayne and I could stay in touch with you." Okay, so my tone was patronizing, but she didn't have to get so huffy.

"How can I check the messages on the machine if you've got the phone line tied up with that thing?"

"You are *so* technologically challenged. It doesn't have to be plugged into the phone jack for you to play back Momma's messages." The fight we'd started yesterday could continue; all it needed was the right needle sliding into the right sore spot.

"Well, excuse *me*, Princess Poot. You're not, I repeat, *not* getting a fight out of me today. I'm too tired to tangle with you."

I felt a stab of guilt. Not my first and, I knew, not my last. Good Protestant guilt makes my world go around. "I'm not fighting with you, either." I sounded churlish, even to myself.

Earlene spun the dial on the antiquated answering machine and we were treated to the high, whining sound of rewinding audio tape. Lots of messages.

"That Jack Shepherd guy is here. He just described Miss Carlotta as 'a nice old lady.' Can you believe that?"

"Nice to a good-looking younger guy, maybe." Earlene almost winked. She punched a button.

"Hellooooo, you have reached the residence of Audrey Moore Hudson. Sorry I'm not here to take your call, but I dooooo want to hear from you, soooo, leave a message after the tooooone."

My sister and I stared at each other.

"God, Early, that is creepy. Hearing Momma's voice and knowing she's dead." I was whispering. "It's like hearing a ghost."

Earlene nodded. "When I first got the news from Wayne, I came over here and played it over and over again. I just wanted to hear her voice. I don't know why, I just wanted to hear her."

She pulled the stool over to the counter and wearily perched herself on it. "Then I cried for about an hour. Just sat here at the table and cried and cried." She leaned back and closed her eyes. I could tell how exhausted she was from the blue circles under her eyes. "I still can't quite believe she's dead, Carrie. Sometimes I accept it, and then the next second, I'm shaking all over."

"It hasn't sunk in with me, either." I pulled out my cigarettes and offered her one. She took it, lighting it with a wooden kitchen match from over the stove.

"After all the effort I put into quitting. The patches, going to that hypnotist over in Salisbury. Eating my way through a two-pound bag of Junior Mints. All it takes is one piece of big stress like this and I'm smoking again." She made a face, then squashed the cigarette out in the spoon rest beside the stove. "Momma would kill me if she caught me smoking in her house."

"And yet she'd let any old guy who came down the pike sit right here and puff away like a troll under a bridge. Tobacco, dope, crack, I don't think it mattered to her, as long as it had a penis and a pulse."

Earlene bit her lip. "Don't speak ill of the dead, Charmaine. She was your mother."

"I can't argue with that. But biology is not destiny."

"You are such a bitter, disappointed child," my sister informed me. Happily for both of us, the messages started to play at that moment, distracting us from picking up where we'd left off with last night's fight.

"Hey, is anyone there?" Wayne's voice crept from the machine, uncertain. He never was comfortable on the phone. "I've been waiting and waiting for Delmar to show up. You said he'd be here by two, and it's two-thirty now and I don't know if I'll get another phone call today. This place is really weird." He waited, as if hoping someone would pick up. "Okay," he said with a deep sigh, ever put upon. "If Delmar calls up there, tell him to ask for airport security when he gets in. They know where I am. I'm not happy here!"

"Oh, I just bet he's not," Earlene snapped, mashing the button. "That must have been yesterday."

"That is so typical Wayne," I pointed out. "Panics if a plane's late but has no concept that he caused all the trouble. He's just lucky we didn't leave him there."

"Or that Delmar could get a flight to Miami on short notice. I don't want to tell you what that cost us first and last. We're just fortunate Delmar was able to get there, instead of you."

I opened my mouth to ask just what she meant by that, then decided that I knew *exactly* what she meant and she was dead-on right. I would have made rescuing Wayne even worse than it already was, and old Romilar probably would *still* have to go down there and straighten things out.

"Hey, Early, honey, it's Delmar." His voice sounded soft and reluctant. Delmar was a man of few words at the best of times. "I'm down here, and I've spoken to Wayne and to the airport security people. Tried to call you at home and over to the View 'n' Chew, so I thought I'd try here. It's about seven o'clock, and it looks as if this is going to be a little more complicated than I thought. Well, you know what Wayne's like. We have a court hearing tomorrow, and if I can get Wayne straightened out through that, we should be home in a couple of days. Love ya, honey."

"Well, there you go, that's last night," Earlene said. She picked up the squashed cigarette and relit it, inhaled, then crushed it out again. She *was* stressed out.

There were a couple of messages for Momma from people who hadn't gotten the news yet, which was sort of creepy, and a couple of messages for us from people who had heard and were wondering when the funeral was.

"The obituary won't even be in the paper until tomorrow and people already know! There are no secrets out here," I whined. "Don't you see what I mean about this town?"

"Of course I know what you mean. And that's why I don't want you talking about Momma being eaten by an alligator!"

"The thing is, she would love it! She loved attention—she'd do anything to get it. She would be thrilled to death that she was the talk of the town! And if it was just a shade exaggerated, she'd like that even better."

Earlene slid off the stool. She poked her finger into the Oasis in the flower arrangements, then ran the sink tap into the containers. "These are as dry as a bone," she muttered to herself. "You'd think she'd have enough sense to put a little water in these containers before she delivered 'em." Gingerly, she lifted the carnation-laden arrangements and took them into the living room.

"I don't think Momma would want to be remembered as a fool, Charmaine." Her voice drifted back to me. I sensed, rather than saw her fussing with the baker's fern and the baby's breath.

"But she was a fool, Early, a woman who should have known better and still made stupid decisions that hurt other people."

"Maybe so, Carrie, but getting your revenge on a dead woman is pretty useless. All you can hurt now is the family. And I think we've been through enough." Earlene returned to the kitchen. She took a sponge and a bottle of cleaner from beneath the sink and began to spritz and wipe down the counters. "We don't want ants," she explained. "All these crumbs . . ."

"Revenge? You think I want revenge on Momma? And you call *me* dramatic?" I stared at a collection of South of the Border

barware, circa 1960. Did I really want to bid $110 for eight mar-
tini glasses and a shaker, no matter how campy?

"It takes more courage to try and keep this whole thing low-
key and tasteful than to make Momma even more of a—a character than she already was."

"That's very Christian of you," I replied dryly. "Something
you learned at church?"

"No. I don't think it's up to us to try to interpret our opinions
as one and the same with God's will. We need to let Momma go
beyond our judgment now. At least I do." To my surprise, my
sister didn't rise to the bait. She did light that bent-up cigarette
one more time and took a huge drag, then another, allowing the
smoke to dragon out her nostrils. "And there's a lot to let go of."
She mashed the message button again. "Looking to get back at
a dead woman is pretty useless. And it makes us look tacky."

Well, I had plenty to say about what difference did it make
whether anyone thought we were tacky or not, but the answering machine whirred into action again.

"Hey. Anybody there?" Pause. "Hello? Audrey, are you
home yet? Anybody there? Did I call the right number? Audrey,
where are you? I waited as long as I could. Now I'm headin'
home. I don't know what else to do." Then a dial tone.

"Who was that?" I asked.

Earlene shrugged and punched another button. "Wednes-
day, eleven-thirty A.M.," announced the robo voice.

"I have no idea. It sounded kind of like Alonzo Deaver. Isn't
that silly? I must be tireder than I thought."

"It's no wonder. Alonzo escaping from jail is the other big
news in town."

"And hopefully, it will make the gossip about Momma die
down. Alonzo's probably halfway to Mexico right now."

"Hey, Earlene, how are you feeling?" Bearing a snapdragon
and daisy arrangement lodged in a wicker basket, Jack Shep-

herd let himself in the back door. As I watched, stunned, he pecked Earlene easily on the cheek, just as sweet as you please. Apparently the man had insinuated himself into every Oysterback nook and cranny. Earlene pecked him back, which was even stranger.

"I'm holding up." My sister dug into the flower arrangement and found the plastic card holder. "My back and my feet are killing me. It's stress. Business has been slow."

"For us at the Blue Crab, too. It's the hot weather. The florist left these with Mrs. Hackett." He held up the flowers for my sister's inspection. "She's got some wonderful old photographs from the days in World War II when they had all these German POW's picking fruit around here. Now it's all corn and soybeans, but back then, everyone grew fruit. These guys look pretty happy for prisoners. But I guess they were just relieved that they weren't on the Russian front, and they were treated fairly well, three hots and a cot."

In all the years I'd known Miss Carlotta, never one word about her girlhood on a farm, let alone memories of German POW's picking fruit.

"Oh, look, it's a card from Wayne's teacher at the genius school. Isn't that nice? I'd forgotten all about the genius school."

"I bet Wayne wishes he could forget all about it. That's when his life started going downhill."

"What's the latest from Delmar?" Jack was making himself right at home, pulling glasses down from the shelf, filling them with ice and sliced lemon, pouring iced tea from the pitcher in the refrigerator as if he lived here. Which, I suddenly reminded myself, he did, sort of.

In reply, Earlene hit the button.

"Hey. Anyone there? I tried over to the store and the line's been busy all day." Delmar's slightly puzzled voice rose from the box. "They took a hearing on Wayne this morning, and he has to stay in jail for a couple of days 'til the lawyer can get here. Wayne has this prepaid lawyer friend, some man from Key West who sounds like a real character. I'll tell you what, *everyone* down there looks like a real character and I'm running out of high school Spanish. I'll call tomorrow and let y'all know what happens when the lawyer gets here. I wish this had happened closer to home, where we at least know people. Honeybunch, if you're there, I love you and I can't wait to come home. If you need me, call the hotel. 'Bye now."

"Yeah, if he'd pulled that number up here, everyone would know him, and know he's harmless. It wouldn't be the first time he's gotten into some foolishness here. Besides," I just had to add, "Momma used to date Judge Findlay Fish. She woulda gotten him outta this, just like she got him out of everything else."

"Charmaine, please don't jerk my chain right now——"

"Why don't we all go sit on the back porch?" Jack suggested. "There's a little bit of a breeze off the river out there."

He was right; it was a lot cooler out there than inside the house. We settled on the glider, the three of us, lined up like iced-tea-sipping vultures, staring out across the marsh at the fading afternoon light. In the garden, Momma's tomatoes were hanging off the vines, overripe, but I was too hot to even think about picking them.

"Oh, feel that." Earlene sighed, lifting her head to the air. "With that grill going all day long in the View 'n' Chew, I can hardly feel the air-conditioning at all."

"Momma never did like air-conditioning. She was never hot." I sipped my iced tea. "I read somewhere that femmes fatales are always cold. It was a book about Mary, Queen of Scots, I think. She was always complaining about being cold. And so was Momma, so I guess that means Momma was a femme fatale."

"Tell me," Jack asked after a brief but potent silence, "what's the name of that gut out there that winds through the marsh and on out to the river?"

"That's Crazy Sister Creek." Earlene kicked off her shoes and wiggled her bare toes gratefully. "I used to tell Carrie when we were little that it was haunted by these two crazy sisters who chopped up people and used them for crab bait."

"And I believed her! For years after that, I'd sleep with the blankets up over my head." I swatted at a mosquito that had landed on my leg. They use airplanes to spray the marsh, but nothing can completely kill the Maryland State Bird.

"It's just a gut, a narrow shallow little creek winding through the marsh. The loneliness out there can make you crazy. Named after some long-ago pioneer woman who went bonkers out on the marsh."

"And now Earlene and I are the crazy sisters."

"The crazy sisters. Isn't that the truth." Earlene let out a little gust of a sigh. "Someone's got to pick Momma's tomatoes, I guess. They're going to rot on the vine. We could use 'em over at the store."

"Let 'em rot," I advised, putting a hand on her shoulder lest she go then and there to harvest Momma's Best Boys. "Let this whole place go back into the marsh. Let the crazy woman have it."

"You don't understand anything, Carrie." Earlene wasn't being mean. She was just being honest for a change, but I bristled anyway and probably would have started something about then if the phone hadn't rung inside the house.

"That's Delmar," Earlene said as she heaved herself off the glider and slipped into the house. In a second, we could hear her voice as she spoke to Delmar, a married-people conversation, too low to eavesdrop on.

After a while, Jack glanced at his watch. "Whoa! Gotta go!

Tonight's poker night at Ferrus's house. Don't wait up for me."

Poker night. Ferrus's house. The only other thing you could possibly need for total social acceptance in Oysterback would be jumper cables.

And yet, in his presence, Earlene and I had gotten through almost two hours without a fight.

8

The Early Bird
Catches the Stuff

The one thing I hate about what I do is the hours. By nature, I'm a night person. But the nature of the antique business is to be up and at 'em at the crack of dawn. I don't make these rules, but if I want to make a living, I have to abide by them. The competition is murder, and if I'm not there with everyone else, then I'll miss something, because you can bet that someone else will pick it up.

I tiptoed around the kitchen in the dark, making coffee and looking among the foil-covered platters, hoping for some tasty breakfast pastry. This morning, the sad feeling, as gray and heavy as a lead sinker, that I'd been carrying around ever since Momma died, seemed a little lighter.

I knew Jack Shepherd was crashed out on the daybed in the Florida room again, because his snoring was shaking the house. While the coffee perked, I went upstairs and used the bathroom.

On my way out, I passed the closed door of my mother's bedroom, and gave way to temptation. I went in. The smell of my mother, her perfume, her clothes, assaulted me like a smack in the face. The lead sinker feeling returned in triplicate.

I flipped on the light and looked around. It looked as if

Momma had just stepped out and would return any second. The old Victorian bed with its high carved headboard occupied most of the room, while the matching Eastlake dresser and chest of drawers managed to swallow up the rest. Momma's bedroom tastes ran toward the sort of frilly Victoriana that would have done a bordello madam proud, or so we used to tell her. It still embarrassed me, all those smoky pink satin lampshades, fringed cushions, and silk coverlets. I wonder how Daddy put up with it all those years.

One of Momma's suitcases lay open on the bed, and some clothes she'd decided not to take with her were neatly folded on top of the pink satin duvet. There was a spill of bath powder on the floor.

If Earlene had tossed the place, I couldn't tell, but Momma was always sort of messy. Nonetheless, I had to know, even though I really didn't want to know, so I crept across the room and opened the glove drawer in the bureau. My own reflection, pale and unhappy, gazed back at me from the enormous mirror as I rooted around beneath the stack of handkerchiefs. My fingers felt the sharp edges of the jewelry box and I pulled it out. Like most things owned by Momma, it was a confection, lavender silk trimmed with gold. When I opened the lid, it triggered the music box that played "Lara's Theme" while a tiny plastic ballerina spun around and around, a little creaky and crippled now, as if she had arthritis, but still twirling after all these years.

I peeked inside. The pearls were still there, and the pavé diamond earrings and my father's ruby class ring. If Earlene had helped herself to anything, I didn't miss it right off. I was about to lift the tray out when I heard someone behind me.

"Good morning," Jack Shepherd said. He was standing in the doorway, looking half awake, but I felt as if I had been caught stealing something, and quickly slipped the box back in the drawer. "You're up early," he continued, and went into the bathroom.

I snuck out of the room and down the stairs. I wasn't sure why I felt I'd been caught at something, but I did. Maybe it was because I'd made such a big deal about not caring what Earlene took, and there I was, snooping. Of course, I wasn't going to take anything, was I?

While I was at it, I checked in the dining room, and I did notice that the silverware was still in the drawer and my grand-mother's tea set was in the china closet where it always sat, although everything was pretty tarnished. Momma was not big on polishing, either.

Since that took care of pretty much everything of traditional value that Momma owned, I was at a loss to figure out what Earlene might have pilfered, if anything.

Unless, I thought as I sat down and started to pick through the classified ads of yard sales listed in the paper, my sister had been sneaking out funeral cakes and casseroles, as Desiree had sug-gested. With two great big, lazy boys to feed, tuna-noodle casseroles, fried chicken, and Jell-O molds would go a long way. This stuff was going to go bad if someone didn't do something with it and soon. It looked like Miss Havisham's bakery in here.

I was circling the more interesting yard sales when Professor Shepherd appeared, minimally more aware, lurching for the coffee.

"People sure did bring a lot of food," he observed, once he'd poured coffee and the caffeine started to hit. "I never saw so much food coming into a house before. I wrapped up a lot of it and put it in the freezer so it wouldn't go bad."

"When someone dies, or gets sick, everyone brings food over." I circled a multifamily sale over in Patamoke that prom-ised tools and china. You never knew; the tools might turn out to be antiques and the china something other than last week's giveaway from Dollar General. "Don't they bring food where you come from?"

Jack laughed. "Where I come from, no one even knows their neighbors. I was born and raised in the city."

I had to stare at him. "But what about your friends, your family?"

"We used to eat out a lot. No one in my family cooked much. When someone died, we all went out to eat after the funeral. Before the funeral, we'd all have a martini or two. Or three, in the case of my uncle Frank." Jack squinted at a black walnut coffee ring, then cut off a piece. "No one liked Uncle Frank much. In a family of liberal intellectuals, he chose to work in banking and vote Republican. The black sheep, my mother used to say."

"Now, that," I said, indicating the coffee ring, "was baked by Jodi Dachstetter. Fire, flood, famine, Jodi brings a walnut coffee ring. Those black walnuts are delicious but awful hard to crack. She puts 'em in a paper bag and runs over 'em with the truck, then takes a hammer to the shells. It's an awful lot of work, but she says it's a great way to get out your frustrations after a day of standing on your feet waiting on difficult women over to Jodi's Fashion Whirl."

Jack looked interested. "That's something I could use," he murmured. "I never heard that, about cracking walnuts."

"Not just any old walnuts. Black walnuts. They're legendarily tough. That might be why it's bad luck to bring them on board a workboat."

He grabbed a paper napkin out of the plastic holder and scribbled on it: "black walnut . . . workboat, bad luck." Then he looked at me expectantly. "Tell me more."

"More what?" I asked, studying an ad that offered lots of furniture. That could be a bust, or it could be a hoard. Sometimes people didn't know what they had. I circled it with a question mark. It was all the way over toward Route 50, but I could swing past it on my way to Tubman's Corners.

"More stuff like that. About the black walnut."

"Why?" Now I had to look at him. No one wants to know about stupid stuff like black walnuts.

"For the book." He scrawled. "You'd be amazed how much stuff I can pick up just by playing cards with the guys."

"Oh, right. Poker night with Ferrus." I went back to my classifieds.

"Yes. I won twenty bucks. I also lost fifty I couldn't afford to let go. But I learned a lot about the culture of card playing."

"What culture? There's no culture around here, unless you count the community theater over in Patamoke, where the old movie theater used to be. They call it Patamoke Theatre in the Oblong, because the building isn't round."

After some serious internal debate, I selected a piece of blueberry crumble. I was willing to bet that it had come from the kitchen of Miss Sister Gibbs. Her late husband had raised blueberries for years. Just what I needed, a carb-packed breakfast of champions or, at the very least, the *petit déjeuner* of a diabetic in training.

"That isn't the kind of culture I'm writing about." Jack sat down at the kitchen table with his coffee and cake. "I'm writing about the local culture. The things that make this area unique. The folkways, if you will."

I had to laugh. "You mean like elves and brownies and witches and stuff? Momma said that when she was a girl some of the old people still believed in witches, but they weren't very well educated."

I chewed thoughtfully for a moment. "Speaking of Ferrus, some say he's a witch, but he's just mildly prescient. Momma used to say that his mother was a granny woman, a midwife back in the days when women had babies at home. Momma used to say that granny women knew all the spells and roots and berries. But you could say that Ferrus's sixth sense comes with age. After you've seen it all and done most of it, everything becomes predictable, from the weather to human behavior. But I never saw him cast any spells or anything. He's a hard-shell Methodist."

"It's really a pity that no one ever wrote down those old witch stories. The folk belief in witches is so rare these days that you really jump when you see it. Your mother was just starting to tell me about the old granny women when she left for Florida. She was delivered by Ferrus's mother."

It struck me then that maybe I should have paid more attention to Momma, that I'd lost more than a parent; I'd lost a whole world of history, a world I didn't even know existed. I looked at Jack over my coffee, resenting that he knew more about my hometown than I did. "You make this sound like Dogpatch, like some kind of ignorant backwater. I'll admit that it's culturally about two to five years behind the trends, but so is most of America." I was surprised to hear myself defending Oysterback. But I'm a native; I'm allowed to bitch and whine about it all I want. Someone who's not from here cannot; those are the rules. But this guy had broken the rules.

"I really love this place! I'm fascinated by Oysterback. It's unlike any place I've ever lived. That's why I want to write about it. This is my first experience with small-town life. I came out here to rent a slip for the boat and it was like coming home."

"You wouldn't think so if you were raised here," I observed, sipping coffee and debating if it was worth going all the way to Bishop's Head for "some nice old glass" that could turn out to be mayonnaise jars.

"Well, that was one of the reasons I found your mother so compelling. Audrey really knew about this region. All sorts of things. And she had terrific insight into her fellow citizens. She understood why I need to know the etiology of this area."

Memo to myself: look up *etiology*. Meanwhile, I sat there and stared at my mother's last boyfriend. Intellectual arm candy would have been Momma's latest style, since she'd started taking those "adult enrichment" courses over at the college in town. I decided I would keep a weather eye on Jack Shepherd until I found out if he had another agenda no one knew about. One thing for sure, it couldn't be Momma's estate. More worthless junk in one place you never saw.

"So, what are your plans for today that you're up and out so early?" he asked me, peering at the newspaper. "Job hunting?"

I sighed. Lord, give me patience with civilians. "In a way. It's Saturday. Yard sales all morning and then some thrift shops and co-ops. Shore's crawling with stuff, if you know where to look and what you're looking at."

"It's not even five yet! Surely no one will have their yard sale stuff out yet!"

"I'm an early bird. Early birds try to get there even before they put the stuff out, so you can pick over it first. That's how you get the best stuff."

"Early bird . . ." Out came the little notebook. "This is really interesting."

"Oh, there's a whole yard sale culture out there," I promised. "Actually, it's more like a cult. You see the same people at yard sales all the time. They call themselves yard sailors." I spelled that last out for him because I thought it was cute. I glanced up at the Kit-Cat clock. "Look at the time! I've got to get going!"

"Can I come along?" Jack asked. "This sounds like something I could write about."

I was about to say no, but he was so eager, like a puppy that wants to be taken for a ride, that I heard myself saying, "Sure, why not?"

Famous last words. What they're going to put on my tombstone is I KNOW WHAT I'M DOING. Besides, I hate people who are cheerful early in the morning. It's not natural, and it's definitely un-American.

And that was how I ended up driving Jack Shepherd all over the Eastern Shore, with him clutching his notebook in one hand and following me around asking questions. That should have given me a clue, but I was preoccupied with my eternal quest of ferreting out the treasure among the junk.

A thin sullen line of light was just breaking over the trees when we pulled up to the first house. "This looks hopeful," I said, squinting in the murk. "An old house like this usually means some old stuff."

"Who are all these cars?" Jack asked as we parked alongside the road between a couple of vans and a ratty pickup. "I don't even see any lights on in the house."

"Other birds," I explained, "anxious to get first pick. See? These people advertise old tools and china. Old hand tools are really valuable. And there might be some good stuff in among the china."

"They also say women's clothing, linens, toys, baby stuff, and books. And 'lots, lots more.'"

"That's a good sign. It sounds like someone died and they're getting rid of all of her stuff. Sometimes you can pick up antiques and collectibles from what's left over after the family takes what they want. I'm guessing that they've also decided not to have any more kids, because they're getting rid of all their baby stuff and toys, so they decided to toss that stuff into the mix."

Jack rattled the newspaper, peering at the tiny print in the dim light. "You can tell all that just from looking at an ad in the paper?" He reached for his notebook and began to scribble. "Interesting," he said.

That seemed to be his favorite word. *Interesting.* I wondered if he used it a lot with Momma. God knows, one thing she was, was *interesting.* And not always in a good way, either.

Somewhere inside the house, a light went on. "Get ready," I said. "When they start bringing the stuff out, that's our cue to go look. We want to try to get to the stuff before they even take it out of the boxes, see? If you snooze, you lose. Go! Go! Go!"

The minute the lady came out of the garage with a box of stuff, everyone scrambled out of their cars and into the driveway.

An old guy in a baseball cap tried to hip check me away from the man who was dragging two enormous cardboard boxes out of the garage, but I did an end run around him and elbowed my way between two large women in polyester pantsuits.

The man and woman, who looked like a pair of very nice people, stood there gripping their boxes, looking at us as if they were deer caught in the headlights.

The lady tried to clutch her box, but the old guy wasn't having any of it. Before she could stop him, he was rooting through it, mumbling to himself. "Is all that's in here just clothes?" He was highly indignant.

"My great-aunt's dresses—" the lady started to say, but he was long gone, heading into the garage without so much as a by-your-leave, his dirty fingers ripping ceramic objects out of their newspaper wrappings.

"Hey!" the man called, trying to fend off the polyester sisters. "Our ad distinctly said no early birds!"

But we were already inside the garage, right behind the old guy. He smelled like kerosene and unwashed body, but I didn't let that stop me from getting right on top of him and reaching down into the china box. "Outta my way, old man!" I snarled, clawing into the newspaper.

"What are you doing?" Jack Shepherd, out of breath from

trying to keep up, panted behind me. "You people are acting like looters!"

"Old newspaper," I grunted, rifling through the box. "A good sign. Means this stuff has been packed away for a long time. Could be anything in here . . . ah!"

As my fingers closed around something smooth and cold, the old man growled and tried to grab for it, but I was too young and too fast. With a muttered curse, he turned away and began to root through another box.

I examined a flower-painted cup. Turned it over. Occupied Japan. "Bingo." I dove into the box again and soon retrieved eight cups and a chocolate pot in a dainty rose pattern. The old man was examining some ugly gnome lawn ornaments, the kind you could buy at any roadside stand. Dilettante.

"How much for the set?" I asked the lady, who was standing there with her mouth hanging open, watching this plague of locusts tearing apart her carefully packed boxes. "I'll give you ten dollars," I said before she could think of a price. "Amateurs," I hissed to Jack. "Someone with some experience of yard sailing would have marked a price on everything last night."

The lady was determined not to be taken. She got a crafty look on her face as she examined one of the cups. "Twenty-five." She smacked.

"Fifteen." I countered.

"Twenty. These sat for years in Aunt Grace's china cabinet."

The old man was looking at the cups. Just as he opened his mouth to make an offer, I smiled. "Sold."

I knew the old guy was mean enough to tell her I'd gotten the best of her, but I also knew that if he did, it would make it even harder for *him* to get a bargain. He licked his lips, gave me a foul-weather look, and went back to rummaging in the box of plastic pink flamingos and chipped plaster ducks.

The lady started wrapping the chocolate set back up in paper.

"Aunt Grace just loved these, but I never saw her use them. Of course, she was eighty when she died a few months ago. And our house is so small, with the kids and all, and I work, and Bob works, so when do *we* get a chance to use a chocolate set?"

I listened carefully, even as I was eyeing the other boxes and bags of stuff that her husband was doing his best to load onto folding tables in the driveway. Knowing the provenance of your stuff can be helpful in placing it in time and space. "Besides, I'm really not into this old stuff anyway. Our decor is Southwestern, and this really wouldn't fit."

Inwardly gagging, I nodded and agreed politely with her that a rose-painted Occupied Japan chocolate set would really not fit into a decorating scheme that featured coyotes and cacti.

The lady watched with awe as the polyester sisters expertly separated all her late aunt's fine old coats and dresses from the tacky new stuff, building themselves quite a pile. "You know, I think there's some other old china stuff in that box Bob's about to put out on the table. . . . I really don't know what's there, but maybe if you're interested in that old stuff, you ought to look . . ." She handed me a plastic shopping bag with my new possessions carefully wrapped inside. I handed her a twenty-dollar bill, which seemed to please her.

"Put those plastic glasses down, they're dreck, and hold on to these," I said to Jack, thrusting the plastic bag at him. He had the same dazed look as the sellers. Other early birds had begun to join our happy band, and I felt grateful I'd made at least one score before I was literally knocked down by someone stronger and faster who really, really wanted that plastic Tiffany lampshade that really, really looked like a cheap Wal-Mart knockoff. And the old-geezer guy glommed onto the Sydenham ironstone pitcher and bowl set before I had even seen it. "Got any decoys?" he buttonholed the hapless Bob, peeling cash off a roll as big as a Smithfield ham.

"If I did, I'd be savin' 'em for myself," Bob said, panting, as he laid out a vast selection of dingy *Sesame Street* toys on the folding table. Their stuff, I guessed. You just knew Aunt Grace never had any kids young enough to play with *Sesame Street* toys. But I did spot a winner buried beneath a pile of old towels, and came away with some nice hand-smocked baby dresses for a quarter apiece, much to the silent, stewing indignation of the polyester sisters. The tools turned out to be a bust. Old rusty shovels, a couple of Stanley screwdrivers, a forgettable spirit level. The ancient wooden shot box they came in, however, was a different story. That Remington stencil on the side upped the value to where my offer of three dollars (accepted) made it a steal.

"We're runnin' out of time here," I said to Jack. "So many yard sales, so little time. Come on."

We headed back to the van, threading our way through the hordes of latecomers. It was barely daylight.

You snooze, you lose.

"Of course, most people aren't interested in antiques," I explained to Jack as we barreled over the back roads toward Bethel, where several thrift shops awaited me. "Antiques don't show up much in yard sales, because these days everyone knows what they've got. Yard sailors are looking for stuff they can use in their own immediate lives. Kitchen appliances, kids' clothes, cribs, stuff like that, none of which I'm interested in. Most of 'em wouldn't know a Steiff teddy bear from a stiff wire brush."

I'd gotten some good stuff this morning. A *Charlie's Angels* lunch box, some '50s Matchbox cars, a *Star Trek* chess set with all the pieces. "You might think that's all junk, but most of it's a part of someone's childhood," I lectured. "And people, especially boomers, will pay serious money to get a piece of their childhood back."

Jack scribbled away. "Boomers," he mumbled.

It's so flattering to have someone interested in what you do. It makes you feel special. And since I don't spend much time around people, I was enjoying the novelty of having company.

"And what kind of things do they like?" he asked.

"Toys, games, books, anything with TV or movie stars, especially kids' TV stuff. If I could find 'em, anything with Roy Rogers and Dale Evans would move. Hopalong Cassidy . . . cowboys. They love cowboys. And Davy Crockett. And space stuff. Rocket ships and robots and stuff like that."

"Stuff . . ." he muttered, scribbling, and suppressed a yawn. "This getting up early is hard work, you know."

"Wake up! Our day has hardly begun. Things are mostly picked over by now, but we'll stop if we see any more sales."

"We're headed home now?"

"Oh, no! The day's just begun! There are lots and lots of thrift shops all over the Shore, and I intend to hit as many of them as I can. Saturday's the day everyone brings in their stuff, and I want to be the first to pick through it. We've got miles to go before we sleep."

I was so busy talking that I barely noticed the guy standing by the side of the road with his thumb out. I don't pick up hitchhikers, but he did look awfully familiar.

But stuff, and the promise of the unknown treasure, awaited. I stepped on the gas and kept on talking about thrift shop culture.

9

Bad Blood, Bad Blood, Whatcha Gonna Do?

In the twilight of a late-summer day, the harbor at Oysterback didn't look quite as dirty and gritty as it did in the harsh light of noon. The sun setting across the river softened the world so that the white, rust-streaked workboats and the dingy green water looked like a tourist's painting.

At this time of day, the harbor was almost deserted. Just a couple of watermen baiting up their lines on the other side of the cove, and, happily, the wind was blowing in the other direction, so the stench of salted eel wasn't murderous.

It was most peaceful. Not even the mosquitoes were swarming, although someone, somewhere was playing Garth Brooks.

"You can tell a lot about Americans by what they have in their yard sales," I said around a mouthful of Big Mac. "You can tell the ways in which their lives are changing. For instance, if they're selling baby furniture, like cribs and high chairs and baby clothes, it means they've decided not to have any more children. If they're selling lots of household goods, like pots and pans and curtains and stuff, it often means they're getting a divorce. If they're older, selling off furniture and bric-a-brac means they're moving to a smaller house. Empty nesters tend to get rid of the junk their kids didn't take—sports equipment, books, clothes, dolls, CD's—and records. There's a whole market out there for vinyl—33's, 45's, 78's—you wouldn't believe. I know a couple of guys who specialize in old records. See 'em around, here and there, and all they look at are the old records—a mint copy of *Blonde on Blonde* is worth like a thousand dollars . . ."

Jack finished off the last of his fries and leaned back against the cockpit of his boat. In the long summer twilight, with the sun setting over the harbor behind him, he looked right at home. He had a pretty nice sailboat, a Triton 36. It was old, but you could tell that he'd done a lot of work on it. His galley and his head were both very clean, and the teak on the deck was well oiled. I gave him points for that. Since I live in a small space, I know what a hassle it is to keep everything clean and organized.

After a long day that had taken us up and down every two-lane blacktop on the Shore, just sitting still by the water was especially peaceful. I was still trying to get the smell of dead people's polyester clothing out of my nose, but that's an occupational hazard. Besides, I'd turned up a Roseville bowl, a handful of vintage Monet costume jewelry, and a Madame Alexander Cissy doll, circa 1970s, that hadn't been loved into a wreck yet. Not a bad haul. I was feeling pretty good, nattering on a mile a minute on the one subject I actually knew something about.

"What are you smiling at?" I asked. Then I noticed that he'd finished off his entire Value Meal, while I'd been talking so much I'd barely eaten half my burger.

"You certainly know what you're doing," he told me. "I've learned more about your world today than I've learned about Oysterback in a month."

I shrugged. "It's been a good day. I glommed up a lot of good stuff. It makes me feel good, really good, when I come home with the van loaded up. You brought me some luck."

"That's a very romantic view. You worked bloody hard and logged a lot of miles today. I've seen parts of the Shore I didn't even know existed before. And I enjoyed listening to you explain it all. This has been an interesting experience for me, learning more about the culture." Scribble, scribble in the notebook.

"I don't get a chance to talk about it much. I travel alone, and I live alone, and the people I mostly hang out with are pickers like me, so I don't have to explain anything to them because they already know. And no one else has ever been interested before. It's sort of neat, when you get to talk about it."

"The thrill of the open road, the thrill of the chase. You're quite the hunter-gatherer, Carrie."

I had to look at him to make sure he wasn't laughing at me. Around here, not too many people get the point of what I do, much less why I do it. But he seemed sincere about it.

"You've got your high-enders and your low-enders. Some days, when things are going really well, I feel like the queen of the high-enders. I guess you're a hunter-gatherer too," I offered, looking around his neat sailboat. "You collect information. And you're ready to roam, in this boat. You could pick up and sail to anywhere. You could go anywhere and write your book. Some tropical island down in the Caribbean."

"That's what I think about. When it starts getting cold, I'm outta here for the winter. Plus, my unemployment will run out then. I'll sail down the Inland Waterway and on to a place in the Caicos called Big Pig Cay. Drink rum drinks and listen to steel bands. Get a leg up on the book I want to write. Live on my severance pay all winter and hope I can find a publisher. Maybe, if I get published, I'll find I can make a living writing." He grinned. "And pigs will fly."

"Yeah. I heard you didn't get tenure. What was up with that?"

If I had dropped a flaming bag of dog doo into his lap, I couldn't have gotten an unhappier reaction. "Well, they had to cut back the history department's funding to make room for the Billy Chinaberry Institute of Poultry Studies." He swirled the ice in his drink. "And I made the mistake of telling the new college president that academic credibility was not built on large corporate checks. I guess the cradle socialist was coming out in me, but it pissed me off that something as basic to a liberal arts education as the study of local history was being ignored in favor of a chicken magnate's massive ego." He suddenly grinned. "And I'd had a couple of beers at the reception. And your mother had organized a protest, getting a few of the kids to show up wearing chicken suits, and I think that was what really pissed off my department head."

"I should have known Momma was involved in this somehow." What does it say that I wasn't one bit surprised that Momma'd show up somewhere wearing a chicken suit?

"Well, they were just waiting for me to do something they could actually pin on me, point out that I wasn't marching in lockstep, and I just made it easy for them. I guess I'm not cut out to play academic politics. I just wanted to teach history, preferably local history. What was it Bernard Shaw said? Something about the reason intellectual infighting is so bitter is because the stakes are so low? And yeah, I resent the whole trend toward letting corporate fat cats like Chinaberry stick their names on everything. Old Main is now AOL Hall, for God's sake. Now they've started to dictate what I can and can't teach. How can you teach local history without mentioning that the poultry industry around here has a history of exploiting employees, growers, and anyone who cares about the Bay? Where do you think all that chicken shit ends up? Right here in the water!"

Everyone has a hot-button topic, and evidently I'd found

Jack's. He was certainly good-looking when he was aroused, his eyes sparkling, face animated, chest all puffed out, his Coke cup waving around in the air like a banner. I could see why a woman would find him attractive. Passion is always alluring.

"I can see why Momma found you, uh, so interesting." I wiped my greasy fingers on a napkin.

"Your mother felt she'd really contributed to my termination. And maybe she did, but if you'd seen her out there in that chicken suit in front of the AOL building, leading those kids, you would have been proud of her."

"Not necessarily. And Earlene probably would have shot herself right then and there."

"But you know, as dramatic and impulsive as she could be, Audrey was *never* dull," he continued as if he hadn't heard me. "And she felt so bad, she opened up her house to me and helped me get that job with Desiree and took me around and introduced me to everyone and convinced them to let me do their oral histories for my book. She more than made up for it. And she pointed out to me that I was miserable at the college anyway. You teach for enough years and you burn out, looking at the same bored kids year after year. You don't want to be there at eight o'clock on a Monday morning and neither do they. If it weren't for her, I'd probably still be living in a two-room apartment and taking Prozac and trying not to fall asleep in faculty meetings. Audrey let me out of jail!"

"That's good. I'm glad she helped someone."

I think Jack could tell by the tone of my voice that I wasn't terribly thrilled with her, chicken suit or no chicken suit.

"There's something else I don't get," I said. "If you're such a liberal socialist or whatever, what do you *see* in these people around here? Most of them are rigidly conservative, more out of a fear of outsiders than any real political conviction. I'd say they don't like blacks, tourists, gays, Catholics, Jews, and uppity women, except their prejudices are more universal; they don't like *anyone* not from here. Sometimes I think they don't even like each other. Oysterback doesn't much care for people from Patamoke, and people from Patamoke look down on folks from Tubman's Corners. So how did *you* worm your way into everyone's good graces?"

"Ah, that's because you are seeing this place and these people through your own prejudices!" I had the feeling he'd delivered a teaching point. "You know, you all have a really interesting town out here on the marsh. It has still maintained many of its unique customs and culture after three hundred years. The kinship ties are especially interesting."

"This is just a high place in the marsh, miles from anywhere else. The tourists come out here and tell us how cute and quaint all these weatherbeaten old buildings are, how the old folks speak a dialect of old English that goes back to the seventeenth century. How Oysterback is supposed to be this wild and lawless place where we cut you if you stand, and shoot you if you run. And maybe it was, hundreds of years ago. Now grass grows in the streets."

"See? A totally jaded worldview." He looked at me over his glasses. "That's what attracted me to Oysterback in the first place. I've done some research, you know."

"About the witches and the maroons and the pirates?"

Jack looked surprised. "You know about that?"

"Of course. We learn it in school. Everyone knows about that. Oysterback was settled by all these folks in the 1600s who had to hide out in the marsh, a place so desolate and hard to get to that the rest of the world wouldn't come after them. People called us Eckies, after an Indian chief named Eckie whose tribe found the place way back when. A couple of women accused of witchcraft running for their lives, a lot of escaped slaves, pirates

on the lam from the law—people on the run were our ances-
tors. Everyone had a good reason to get to a place where no one
could catch them. It became a sanctuary, with its own laws and
customs. Everyone used to be ashamed of that. Then they got
all respectable, or what passes for it around here. It's only
recently that folks have started being proud of who we are. Now
they have the Mosquito Festival once a year and make money
to support the fire department. It's like a big 'Yeah, We're
Quaint, Now Give Us Money' party."

"Ah, yes, the Mosquito Festival. A celebration of West Hundred heritage. I've not only been, I was asked to run the Story-
teller's Booth, where you entertain folks with local lore. The
kids loved the story about the Harbeson brothers. You know,
Levin chopped up Daniel and salted him down for crab bait,
but Daniel's ghost came back and—"

"I know the story, probably better than you do."

His smile said "I doubt that," but I pressed on.

"The Mosquito Festival is the one day we don't call people
born somewhere else 'foreigners,' 'come-heres,' or 'blow-ins.'"

"Smile when you say that!" Jack laughed, clearly and maddeningly delighted by my anger. He leaned forward. "When
the festival planning committee met down at the fire department, Huddie Swann said to Junie and Omar, 'Well, it's the one
day we like the foreigners to come here.' Then he turned to me
and said, 'Oh, I don't mean you, Jack. You're just not born here,
but you're one of us.'"

"Well, I was born here and I couldn't wait to get away. Did
you notice that in small towns like this, the median age is about
fifty-five? That's because anybody with any ambition, any
sense, any desire for a more interesting life gets out as soon as
they can. Growing up in a small town is like being in high
school for the rest of your life. Everyone looks at you, looks at

your family, and decides you're going to be just like your mother. You'll never escape that, not ever. Why do you think Earlene is so desperate to be a pillar of the community?"

I didn't like the way he was writing in that notebook again. I suddenly realized I'd said more than I intended, that I'd exposed my own weakness to someone who might have the power to wound me. It made me really angry.

To defend myself, I went on the attack. "About that book. How long do you think it will take to finish it? You know, you're like everyone else around here. That's why they like you. You're hiding from the world, just like they are."

I may have only a couple of years of college to my credit, but I've heard the hoot owls hoot in enough places to know exactly the worst question to ask a wannabe writer, a defrocked professor.

It seemed to have worked. He looked sightlessly around the harbor, staring at the other boats, and ran a hand over his beard, squinting uncertainly. "Well, that's a good question," he muttered. "I'm not really certain. In a couple of weeks, I'll be as far away from that damn college as I can reasonably get on a limited budget." He grinned. "Ever been to the islands? You might enjoy it."

It was as if God had snapped His fingers and declared the scene was over. I suddenly stood up, brushing McDonald's crumbs from my shirt. I looked at his watch. "Is it really that late?" I asked. "Boy, we've been up for a long time, and I still haven't put in a funeral plan today."

He could take a hint. I wasn't terribly surprised when he added, "I think I'll stay on board tonight. I have a lot of notes to transcribe."

"Sure." I got up. "Well, it was fun. I'll see you around."

Jack looked at me over his glasses. "You know," he said quietly, "for some people, Oysterback is a place to run to, not away from. It all depends on how you look at it, what you bring to it."

"One woman's hell is another man's haven," I muttered, and climbed out of the boat and stepped onto the dock.

I'd just started the van when I heard someone knocking on the window and turned to see Jack with his face pressed up against the glass. I rolled down the window.

"Look," he said quickly, "I'm sorry. I didn't mean to be rude or pushy. I just thought if you were in the mood to travel, you might wanna think about it . . ."

I swear he was blushing.

I nodded. "That's all right. We're all kind of tense about everything that's happened. I know you didn't mean anything."

"Thanks for understanding." He touched my arm briefly, cocking his head to one side. "I'll see you around, okay? Maybe we can do some more fieldwork before I leave next week."

"Sure," I agreed.

He turned and walked back to the boat, jumping over the side with one long stride. And I drove away.

"What is wrong with you?" I asked myself aloud, and was not surprised to hear my mother's tone of voice coming out of my mouth. "He's a perfectly nice guy. Even with the Momma thing . . ."

Even though you swear that you will never, ever be anything like your mother, sooner or later bits and pieces of her will manifest themselves in you when you least expect it.

She'll never die as long as I'm alive; I'll carry her around in my head for the rest of my life, reminding me that in her eyes, I will always be less than perfect. Less than Earlene. Because I am manless, homeless, and rootless.

It was a terrible thought. I wanted to take my brain out and dry-clean it to get rid of every trace of her. Along with every urge to go back and ask Jack more about his sailing plans.

Oh, well, I thought, no longer my problem, and hearing my stash of new treasures rolling around in the back of the van as I bounced down the road, I cheered up immediately. I was looking forward to going home and playing with them, entering them into my log, examining them at my leisure and figuring out which of my clients might buy what. And for how much.

As soon as Wayne and Delmar got back, I would be so out of here and back on the road.

10

The Clot Sickens

The minute I pulled up in the driveway, I knew it was not to be. Earlene's lead sled was sitting there, high, wide, and gas guzzling. And just like you can feel a storm coming in over the Bay, I could sense that our truce was over and she was in a mood. But then, when is she not? Earlene got stuck in mental menopause about the age of eighteen and will probably be there until the day Parsons Dreedle nails the coffin lid down on her, and I doubt even then she'll shut up.

Sure enough, my sister looked like thunder, sitting at the kitchen table with her arms crossed over her chest and all the diamonds in her rings glittering. Yet more funeral food was spread out all around her, and the house smelled like a greenhouse. I didn't have to look in the living room to know more funeral flowers had arrived.

"Where have you been?" were the first words out of my sister's mouth.

"Hello would have been nice," I replied, washing my hands in the sink so I didn't have to look at her sour face.

"Well, Parsons Dreedle and I sat here for two hours waiting for you to show up, Carrie." I had a feeling that if looks could kill, I'd have a big hole in the back of my head. "And after he gave up and went, I've been sitting here all alone, with an escaped convict roaming around."

"Well, if you'd told me Parsons was coming, I would have been here." I dried my hands carefully, trying to keep my tone reasonable. "Unfortunately, you didn't. And Alonzo, no doubt, is halfway to California by now. Why would he come back to Oysterback? He's dumb, but he's not a masochist."

The creases running from Earlene's nose down to the sides of her mouth deepened as she set her lips in that tight little line. "I did so tell you. I told you yesterday when you got in that he was coming at two to discuss the funeral."

"That's very nice of Alonzo, but I think we can manage on our own."

Okay. Now, if you've been following me so far, you know as well as I do that she never said boo about Parsons. You also know that I just stuck the knife into my own sore spot with that smart crack, which my sister was in no mood to hear.

"That's right, make a big joke out of it. Everything is one big joke to you, isn't it. Well, it's funny only because you don't have to take any responsibility for anything!"

Slowly I turned. "Earlene, you never said anything about this to me. You might have told someone, but it wasn't me, or I would have been here."

"I sat right here and told you, Carrie. Right here in this chair."

"No. You didn't tell me. And now you want to pretend that you did so I'll look bad and you'll look like the suffering martyr."

I lit a cigarette and noticed my hands were shaking.

It tasted really bad, but I needed something to do so I didn't slap her skinny ass off the chair. "You can give it up, Earlene. Momma's dead. There's no one here to come beat me up for something you made up. She's dead, Earlene, and she's not going to rise from the grave to back up one of your cheesy lies this time, so get the hell over it!"

Okay, so I lost it. I fell for the bait and lost it, just like she wanted me to.

"Oh, you think you're so smart, don't you? Momma, not cold in her grave, and you talkin' bad about her! She was right about you—you *are* an ungrateful little bitch!"

"Well, she was right about you, too! You're a whiner and a liar and a hypocrite."

I guess she'd gotten what she wanted, because that thin little mouth turned up in a grim smile. "You just couldn't stand that I was her favorite, could you?"

I closed my eyes, took a deep breath, and had, for once in my life, a clear thought. "Listen, Earlene, what is this really all about? Because I'm sick and tired of going over the same damn issues with you, over and over and over again."

"Ooooh, the gloves are off!" Well, if she wanted a fight, I could give her one. And without Momma there to take up for her, it might even be a fair one. "Well, so what if Momma was hard on you?"

"After Daddy wasn't around to protect me anymore. He thought you were a common sorry snitch, just like I do!" I pitched my voice up two octaves. "*Momma, Carrie said a bad word! Momma, Carrie's been borrowing my clothes again! Momma, Carrie called me a tattletale!* Now, that was my favorite!" I exhaled a stream of smoke.

Earlene stiffened. "Well, you were so out of control, I had no choice. Daddy let you get away with murder!"

"Did not!"

"Did so!"

I stood up and leaned across the pastry-laden table. I was getting Marmalade Upside-Down Cake all over my shirt, and I didn't care. "Dammit, Earlene, you make me so mad I could spit! Where the hell were you when Momma had Dog livin' here and he was chasin' me all over the place with his damn dick hanging out of his pants like a turkey neck? Momma may not have believed me when I told her, but Jesus Christ, you walked in and saw him and never did a damn thing about it! What were you thinking? Why didn't you do something? You were the oldest! She would have believed you!"

Earlene's face crumpled like a collapsed soufflé, but she hung in there. "I don't know what you're talking about," she said, all stiff. "I was married and out of the house. I never saw anything like that."

"You'd rather have a hysterectomy with a rusty spoon than admit you've ever been wrong, wouldn't you? Don't deny it. You saw what was happening here! I know you did! And you didn't do anything. Do you really hate me that much? I was just a kid, Earlene! Just a kid!"

I have no idea what got into me, but I snapped. I could feel it in my head, as if someone had taken a scissors and cut the last ties I had to civilized behavior.

It was right there in front of me, so I picked up Mrs. Elmo Rainbird's banana cream pie and threw it at my sister. I hit her right on the jaw, splattering viscous yellow custard all over her and the refrigerator. "This is for leaving me in this hellhole while you ran off and got married!"

"Oh! Oh! Oh!" Earlene wailed, jumping to her feet so fast she knocked over her chair. She touched some custard on her cheek and got this really nasty look on her face, at least what you could see of it beneath the banana chunks. "You little— b-bitch!"

She grabbed the nearest thing to her, a Pyrex macaroni and cheese casserole dish, and started scooping it out, throwing handfuls of noodles at me. Old Earlene had a mean pitching arm, I have to admit; when that first blob of cold gelatinous goo hit me square between the eyes, I howled. "And this is for showing up stoned at my wedding! You were so high the sash on your bridesmaid's dress was tied in front!"

"Hey, that hurts!"

"It ought to hurt! You know Doreen Redmond couldn't cook her way out of a wet paper bag!" Earlene was jumping up and down now, like a boxer, fists cocked at me as she circled the table, coming after me.

I danced away from her, and picked up a Jell-O mold. If you are going to toss something at someone, there is nothing that makes a more satisfying *plop* than a lime Jell-O, mayonnaise, and mandarin orange combo shaped like a lobster. It landed on the top of her head and stuck into Earlene's frizzy hair as it dribbled down her face. "That's for taking my favorite yellow sweater and losing it on the rides in Ocean City!"

"Ur, ur, ur—" Sputtering, she was blind with rage and Cool Whip. With a sweep of her hand, she started dumping Momma's funeral feast off the table. Dishes crashed to the floor, crockery and china shards rolling everywhere. "I'll kill you, you little brat!"

I picked up a handful of Chocolate Decadence Cake and smashed it into where I thought Earlene's face should be. Cheese sauce in my eyes made it hard to aim. Unfortunately, she moved too fast for me.

"Now look at what you've gone and done, you crazy witch! You've ruined my outfit!" Earlene yelled at me, clutching the back of a kitchen chair as she slid in the mess toward me.

"No big loss, as you have no taste," I snarled, but she nailed me good with a big old chafing dish of Velveeta-stringbean casserole, right upside my head.

"That's for telling Verdley Sheldrake that I padded my bra in seventh grade!"

"Fuck you, you skinny-ass dork!" I yelled, and flew at her

with a plate of ham salad nestled in a bed of iceberg lettuce. I always hated iceberg lettuce.

She was coming back at me with a Crock-Pot of baked beans. We met in the middle of the kitchen floor, skidded on the Jell-O salad, grappled for each other, and went sliding right beneath the table.

"I'm gonna kill you!" I screeched, rolling over on top of her and pinning her face down in her own damn beans. "You told Momma who stopped up the toilet with the brussels sprouts!"

"Not if I kill you first!" Earlene shrieked, and got me good on the back of the head with a fistful of Tomato Surprise, which can really hurt you when it's delivered with a closed fist. "This is for breaking my Add-A-Pearl necklace before the senior prom!"

I saw stars and smelled ginger and brown sugar. When I tried to get a purchase on the floor with my knees, I just slid and fell down again. Beneath me, Earlene was having the same problem. She couldn't get a grip either, which was a good thing, because from the look I could see on her face, she really was mad enough to kill me. I hadn't seen her that angry since I broke her bottle of Vanilla Fields one Christmas.

"You ran off and left me here to deal with her. Do you know what that was like, day after day, year after year, looking after her, cleaning up after her messes, praying people wouldn't find out what she'd done now?" Earlene howling was quite a noise, especially right in my ear. "I could have used some help, you know! But I was stuck baby-sitting Momma while you skipped merrily off. You don't have a husband and kids—you could have helped me out instead of running away like you did."

"If I hadn't run away, I would have killed her or myself or both. I didn't owe Momma jack shit. She didn't even like me. *You* were her special one, Earlene!"

"Why do you think I married Delmar as soon as I graduated

from high school? I wanted to get away from Momma as fast as I could. I could have gone to college, like you did. I could have done a lot more with my life than just run the View 'n' Chew if I'd had some business courses. I could have sold real estate!"

She was breathing hard, spitting her words out like roofing nails. I was about to roll off her when she grabbed me by the hair and pulled me down. She pushed my face right into a big chunk of walnut pecan pie. *Whomp!*

I chewed thoughtfully. It was pretty good pie. Then, when she wasn't expecting it, I pushed her off me and pinched her arm as hard as I could. "That's for pulling my hair." I gasped for air. Gobbling is hard work. "The problem, and we do have a problem, is not you and me, it's Wayne. He was always Momma and Daddy's favorite because he was the only son, the blessed boy and the genius wunderkind—"

That's when Earlene screamed. And Earlene can scream, believe me. She could have worked in those old Hammer horror movies if she'd been around back then. Since she screamed right in my ear, I felt as if someone had thrust a long thin needle into my skull.

"Jesus! Warn me when you're gonna do that!" I yelped, but Earlene wasn't screaming at me; she was screaming at a pair of very dirty, very large men's sneakers we could both see from our position beneath the table. God only knew who was attached to them.

It looked like we had a visitor, and at a most inopportune moment, too.

I do so hate drop-in company.

11

Won't You Come Home, Bill Haley?

Oh, yeah, it was Alonzo Deaver. A little older and a whole lot worse for wear since we graduated from Oysterback High, but Alonzo in the flesh. He looked, not unnaturally, like homemade hell.

"Don't let him get near us, Carrie!" Earlene shrieked, slipping and sliding to her knees, then falling into the greasy icing of Francine Fishpaw's coconut cake as she crashed into a table leg. "He'll rape and kill us right here!"

"Oh, lighten up." I plopped down on the floor and squinted through meringue and baked beans at the guy voted "Most Likely to Do 10–15" by the Class of '75. "What's happening, Alonzo? Long time, no see."

Alonzo peered at us, clearly puzzled. Believe me, even Momma wouldn't have been able to pick us out in a lineup, we were so coated with comestibles.

"Carrie? Earlene? Is that you? Did I come at a bad time?"

"Now, I ask you, Earlene. Is a man bent on rape and murder going to ask you if he came at a bad time?" My sister opened her mouth to scream and I shoved a brownie between her lips. Yeah, I know, a moment on your lips, six months on your hips, but she deserved it.

"Well, yeah, Alonzo, this is obviously not a good moment—but to what do we owe the honor of this visit?"

Alonzo stood there for a minute with his mouth open. "Where is Miss Audrey?" he asked plaintively. "She never showed up."

"Showed up where?"

"I *told* you. At the ron-day-voo. She said she would meet me at the ron-day-voo point. The Lock and Load Motor Inn, on the highway behind the detention center."

Earlene and I looked at each other, horrible, unspoken suspicions being confirmed. My sister moaned, pulling the brownie out of her mouth. "Alonzo, did Momma tell you to escape from jail?"

"Yeah," he replied, nodding. "And then, she said she'd meet me down by the motel, but she never showed up. I don't get it. This was *her* idea. Where is she?" He looked about the room, as if Momma were lurking in the broom closet.

Earlene clapped her hands over her ears. Chicken and dumplings dribbled into her earrings. "I don't want to hear this. I really don't want to hear this. What are the neighbors going to say? What will they say down at church?"

"Well, we're told in the Bible that we're supposed to visit the sick and the imprisoned," I informed her cheerfully. "Tell 'em Momma was doing her Christian duty!"

"I'm not telling them anything," my sister hissed. "Get him out of here!"

Alonzo wrung his hands. "She told me she was gonna help me ex-cape, get me to Florida or somewhere. That's what she told me."

Well, he was too dumb to be making this up, that much both Earlene and I knew from past experience. If Alonzo had been any good at criminal behavior, he wouldn't have been caught so often.

"Are you thinking what I'm thinking?" Earlene asked me, utterly horrified.

"Yes, I am. This is *exactly* the sort of thing Momma would do!"

"Lookee, if you'll just tell her I'm here, Miss Audrey will take care of everything. I know she will." Alonzo kept wringing his hands, looking about himself wildly. "She *said* she would."

It struck me suddenly that he was much more afraid of us than we were of him, which to my mind, made him comparatively more intelligent. "You're gonna have to tell him, Earlene."

"Not me! I'm not having anything to do with this! I cleaned up Momma's messes when she was alive, but this is too much! Call Sheriff Briscoe. Let him deal with it!"

Enlightenment, always somewhere over the rainbow for Alonzo, began to dawn. "Somethin' happened to Miss Audrey, dinnit? I knew there had to be a good reason why she didn't come. She was always so good at showin' up on visitin' day." His face crumbled. "What happened to her? Is she hurt? Did she get into a car accident or somethin'?"

"You'd better sit down, Alonzo." There wasn't an upright chair in the room, so I struggled to my feet and picked one up. "Sit," I commanded, and he sank obediently into it, folding his lanky frame without taking his eyes off my face.

"Momma's passed over." I tried to keep my voice gentle, and tried to keep my distance. His hygiene wasn't too wonderful and became a problem if you were standing downwind of him.

"Oh, Lord," he whispered, and large tears began to track down the dirt on his sad, prison-pallor face. "Oh, poor Miss Audrey!" He collapsed and I suddenly understood what the old people mean when they say someone fell to weeping. He rocked back and forth, with a high, keening sound. It was odd to hear it coming out of a grown man. It sounded more animal than human.

I felt guilty because he was obviously more upset about Momma than either Earlene or me.

"It was like this, Alonzo," I said as I rather reluctantly patted his shaking shoulder. "Momma went to Florida because Wayne was in some kind of a pickle, and while she was there, they went to Gator Gardens, and she fell into the alligator pit."

"She had a heart attack!" Earlene corrected me as she struggled unsteadily to her feet, wiping food away from her face with the hem of her shirt. "Don't you listen to her, Alonzo. Momma had a heart attack! She was *not* eaten by an alligator. We. Are. Not The. Kind. Of. Tacky. People. Who. Get. Eaten. By. Alligators!"

"Oh, I don't know. I'd say we're tacky enough," I mused, looking at Alonzo, the escaped convict, collapsed in grief.

If I'd thought it couldn't get any worse, I was so wrong.

"Her conjugal visits were the only thing that made the past year worth livin'. When that trailer was a-rockin', no one was knockin'. She was a woman and a half!" He convulsed into fresh sobs and didn't see the look on Earlene's face.

"Don't start. Please, I'm begging you, don't start."

Earlene pulled a roll of paper towels right off the rack and began to clean herself up. Her mouth was so tight you couldn't see her lips, which is not a good sign. She methodically sponged goo out of her hair, then off her clothing. She didn't say a word, which scared me even more than her giant fainting hissy fits.

To tell the truth, for once in my life, I was totally without a clue. I felt as if I'd been hit with a stun gun. Some things are not meant for humans to contemplate, and the picture of Momma getting it on with Alonzo Deaver in a conjugal trailer at the prison was definitely on top of that list.

Earlene took a deep breath. She went to the freezer and

pulled out a casserole dish, which she carefully placed in the microwave. "He might as well have something to eat," she muttered, pushing buttons. "He's been through the Momma wringer. No need to let him starve on top of it."

Then she rummaged in the cupboard under the sink. Triumphantly, she retrieved a bottle of Murphy's Oil Soap. Only it wasn't oil soap; it was whiskey. "Another one of Momma's little secrets," my sister said grimly. "Jack Daniel Black Label. Carrie, get down three juice glasses, the ones with the little ducks," she commanded. When I obeyed, she poured each of us a couple of fingers of bourbon.

My sister knocked hers off before I could even push Alonzo's into his limp fingers. She poured herself another shot, holding the glass up in ironic toast. "Here's to Momma."

She slugged it down in one gulp.

Alonzo sniffled.

I stared.

"*You're nothing without a man,*" Earlene quoted bitterly.

12

Fish and Visitors

The tail on the Kit-Cat wall clock twitched out the seconds. Alonzo sat at the table, sniffling tearfully as he hunkered over a heaping plate of Tater Tot and Swedish meatball casserole. Earlene and I just stared at Alonzo eating and blubbering. He rubbed his temple. "I feel one of my sick headaches coming on," he sobbed.

I finished off the last drops of my bourbon and Earlene poured me another. My throat was burning, so I just swirled it around. Funny how those painted glasses suddenly looked garish and out of place. Unreality had given the dear and familiar a whole ugly look, as if someone had turned on a fluorescent light during a drag revue.

My sister shook a cigarette out of my crumpled pack and lit it, blowing smoke out of the sides of her mouth. Cigarettes and whiskey and a wild, wild man! Whoa! I knew Earlene was really stressed out now. Neither tobacco nor liquor had touched her lips in twenty years, not since she took up with that church down the road.

Staring at Alonzo, she narrowed her eyes, and I knew she was thinking hard. "Eat up," she commanded him. "Food will take care of that headache. There's more in the microwave." Say what you will about my sister, and I've said a lot, she believes that feeding people in times of trouble is the best and only right thing to do. If and when Sheriff Briscoe and his crew burst through the door, she'd be fixing them all plates too. And a fresh pitcher of iced tea.

"Poor Miss Audrey," Alonzo sniffled, and shoveled down some more food. "I guess you'd better call the po-lice. I'll go back. Ain't no reason to stay out without Miss Audrey." Alonzo wept and chewed with his mouth open. Not a pleasant sight. Prison dentistry leaves a lot to be desired.

"I guess he's right, Earlene. We'd best call the sheriff. But tell them he's surrendering peacefully. I don't want a SWAT team breaking down the door and shooting up the place. They might mess up my antiques."

"The police?" Earlene seemed to come back from a long way away. She looked around us at the sodden, multicolored mess. "Carrie, we can't have them coming in here and seeing this! What would Momma say? They'll think we're terrible house-keepers!"

"They'll think Alonzo did it," I added. "Although that doesn't seem terribly fair."

"Uh-uh. Well, let's clean it up before we call them. And you, Alonzo, ought to have a shower. There's clean towels in the linen closet in the hall. And toss down those dirty clothes. I'll run them through the washer and dryer. Scoot along, now. It's getting late, and Sheriff and Mrs. Briscoe go to bed early."

Alonzo wiped the last of the casserole off his plate with a piece of bread, then, still sniffing, left the room. We heard his slow footsteps, and his whimper, as he made his way up the stairs to the bathroom.

"Don't forget to use plenty of soap! And toss those clothes down the steps!" Earlene yelled after him. I guess years of rais-ing boys had given her a lot of inside knowledge on male hygiene or the lack thereof.

His only reply was a muted sob. Alonzo was really broken up about this whole thing, you could tell.

Earlene rose unsteadily from the table. Whether it was nerves or bourbon, I couldn't tell, but she had an odd, determined look that I didn't like one bit. She got the mop and bucket out of the closet.

As soon as we heard the water running in the shower, she grimaced. "Listen, Carrie, I don't know what you think, but I do know if we have the police here, everyone will find out what Momma did this time, and it's more than I can bear." She slammed the plastic bucket into the sink. "How *could* she have been such an old fool?"

"That's probably just it. He's a captive audience." I groaned as I struggled to my feet and grabbed the roll of paper towels. Everything hurt, and I was going to have some bruises in interesting places tomorrow. "Although I don't know how she juggled Alonzo *and* Jack Shepherd. I mean, she was, like, sixty-something, right?"

"She was—with Professor Shepherd too?" Earlene looked as if she had finally found the straw that broke the camel's back. "Dear Lord! And he's young enough to be her *son!*"

"So's Alonzo." I wiped blueberry pie off the counter. Those purple stains never come out of Formica. "As she got older, Momma musta started goin' for the boy toys. I can't believe Jack Shepherd—I mean, why? He's like a human being, you know. Normal. At least he *seems* normal, compared to everyone else."

"That's what I thought 'til five seconds ago. Let's hope Jack doesn't show up here tonight too. And I thought he was such a nice man! Help me scrape up those baked beans. There's got to be a piece of cardboard around here. God knows, Momma never threw anything out."

"Including men."

"Including men. Sweet Jesus, what a mess."

•

Out in the marsh, the peepers sang happily and a rail cackled into the humid night. Mosquitoes banged against the screens, and somewhere down the road, someone was watching the Orioles lose another game. In the pantry, the dryer tumbled with a low moan, and the dim light from a now much cleaner kitchen spilled through the screen door.

"The sound of summer," Earlene said with a sigh as she sank into the glider beside me. She smelled of soap and good grooming. "Alonzo's asleep on Momma's bed. Just passed out there, on top of the covers, wrapped in a towel."

"I guess ex-caping from jail and all wore him out." I yawned, beyond bone tired and well into giddy delirium. I was also slightly drunk. "The surreality, oh, the surreality of ugly surprises."

"Put a lid on it," Earlene said, and she yawned too. "We've really got to call the sheriff, Carrie, before it gets too late."

"I scraped all that food off the floor. I've been driving all day." I yawned again; it is contagious. "You call."

Earlene stretched her legs out in front of her, examining the runs in her panty hose. "I'm tired out myself, you know. This hasn't been the easiest day in my life. By the way, I found this on the kitchen counter. Someone put a plate on top of it." She handed me a scrap of paper that said *From Audrey's Kitchen*. It had a picture of a cardinal on it, clinging to a dogwood branch. My mother, the nature lover.

I squinted at my sister's precise round handwriting in the dim light from the kitchen: "Carrie—Be here at 2:00. Parsons is coming to discuss the funeral. E."

"I never saw it. And I think you owe me an apology, Earlene." But I knew she'd never say she was sorry, so I didn't press it. Besides, I was too tired to pick up the fight we'd never finished when Alonzo suddenly appeared.

"I just wanted you to know that I wasn't making it up or playing getcha."

"Okay." I wasn't going to say I was sorry either, but at least we were acting half human toward each other for a change. Suddenly, a light bulb turned on over my head, just like in the cartoons.

"Say, doesn't Alonzo have any family around here? We could call them and have them pick him up."

"Oh, don't be silly! It's our duty to call the sheriff! We're breaking the law, Carrie! We could go to jail for harboring a fugitive! Thanks to Momma, I'll never be able to hold my head up again!"

"For once, I can see your point. Not about holding your head up, but the part about harboring a fugitive. But I have some trouble picturing Sheriff Briscoe throwing the book at us; he's a pretty easygoing guy. And we're a confused and bereaved family. That must count for something."

"You'd think, wouldn't you?" Earlene was bitter. "You'd think instead of dumping all this food on us, someone would have asked to help." She yawned again. "Alonzo had a brother, didn't he? But I think he went to Minnesota or something, years ago."

"They were raised by their grandmother. Remember her? That crazy lady who lived down by Tubman's Corners? She used to wear that aluminum foil hat so that the sonar beams the Uranians were shooting at her wouldn't penetrate her brain and mess with her thought waves."

"The apple doesn't fall far from the tree. Alonzo was in special ed, remember? I don't remember what happened to the parents. I think they were killed in a car accident on Route 50 or something. It was just the Uranus Lady, raising them."

"Hell of a grandmother. She used to stand in the yard and yell at all the yellow cars that passed by. Just the yellow ones.

She thought they were all driven by Satan. Painted their trailer with all these secret symbols and stuff. Said it was the Uranian alphabet. She used to spend time over to the mental hospital in Cambridge now and again. Then Alonzo and his brother would shift for themselves 'til she got back."

"Well, there you have it. He was looking for a grandmother replacement when he took up with Momma. *She* could have had visitations from Uranus if she'd just tried harder."

"Don't be disrespectful of the dead, Earlene."

"Why? She was never respectful of us! Look at the mess she left us to deal with!" Earlene chuckled nastily. She leaned over and whispered in my ear, blowing whiskey breath all over me. "You know what? I'd like to bring her back to life so I could kill her all over again for doing this to us! That's *just* how angry I am, Carrie!"

"Earlene!" I was genuinely shocked.

She leaned back against the glider cushions as if all the air had been let out of her. "Well, that's how I feel. That's how pissed off I am!"

"Watch it! You're supposed to be the sane one," I advised.

"Maybe I'm tired of being the sane one. You and Wayne get to be the crazy ones all the time. It's not fair. Maybe I want to get me a van and travel all over and get away from the store and the boys and hit the open road. I'm sick of people who don't return videotapes, and you have to call them up and whine and threaten to take them in front of a court commissioner, and I'm surely sick of the smell of frying meat, and I'm *definitely* sick of two grown boys still living at home, expecting me to do their laundry and cook their meals while they spend all their time running up and down the road! By now, I thought Delmar and I could take a vacation. Maybe a cruise, instead of working twelve hours a day, seven days a week. I'm sick of worrying that Delmar's going to keel over with a heart attack from his worrying about the bidness all the time. I'm sick of Delmar havin' to go and clean up after Momma. For that reason alone, I'm glad she's dead, Carrie. Delmar and I won't have to drag ourselves out of bed or away from the store to clean up her g.d. messes anymore! This wasn't how I planned to live my life."

"Well, here's your chance, Earlene. Sell the house, take the money and run. We'll bury Momma, and then you and Delmar can take a world cruise right after. The boys can run the store for a while. Go. Just go!" I took a deep breath. "If you guys want to go away, I'll stay and look after the store and ride herd on the boys. I'll get a whip and a chair."

Earlene laughed in the dark. "I believe you mean that, Carrie."

"I do. You're right. I ran. It was my only choice. If I'd stayed around here, I'd be—I'd be wearing an aluminum foil beanie and howling at cars myself."

"You'd be good at that." Earlene was laughing, a deep, gutsy laugh that slid up and down an octave.

"I could steal a shopping cart from the Buy 'n' Bag. Pile all my worldly goods into it and live down to the harbor in my van. Don't pay any attention to her, that's Miss Carrie, the bag lady." I started to giggle, gasping, uncontrollable wisps of laughter. "Everyone would say I was driven mad by Momma!"

In my weariness and hysteria, this thought struck me as unbearably funny and I went off into a spasm of cackling. I couldn't stop, and I couldn't breathe. I could only laugh helplessly. Earlene snorted, then giggled, then collapsed, whooping, against me.

"She was getting stranger and stranger. Desiree banned her from the Blue Crab a few months ago!"

"I can see that now. Desiree pointing toward the door, yelling 'Out!' and Momma threatening to sue her. Dear Lord, what did she do?"

"She . . ." Earlene leaned over and whispered a sordid tale into my shell pink ear.

"She didn't!" I gasped, then roared with laughter, unable to stop the flood of hysteria. I leaned back against the glider, too debilitated to move. Laughter shook me in helpless convulsions, even though I was totally horrified. "At least she got another wearing out of the chicken suit before she took it back to the costume place."

"Momma always did love to be the center of attention," I managed to say between spasms of laughter. "But, my God, she was getting to be worse than Wayne ever was."

Just as we had done when we were kids, and were supposed to be asleep, Earlene and I stuffed cushions against our mouths to stifle the sound. "We don't want to wake up Alonzo," Earlene hissed.

"Or Miss Carlotta. If she comes stormin' over here, we are so much dead meat!"

"D-dead meat!" Earlene went into whoops again.

The moon was rising, a fat chunk of a crescent, over the endless marsh. When I was little, I thought it came up from the distant Chesapeake, rising from the water every night, a silent witness from the depths, watching us all.

Our laughter, stifled and hysterical, painful, helpless, and hilarious, spilled out across the still grasses, the winding creek, penetrating into every hidden place in the wetlands.

It was terrible, this laughter.

"Earlene," I said after a long time, after the hysteria had begun to pass, "suppose we just let Alonzo sleep? Maybe he'll wake up in the morning and take off and it'll be someone else's problem. No one will ever know he was here!"

But Earlene didn't respond. I turned to her. She looked as if she'd passed out, her head thrown back, her mouth half open, sprawled like a cast-off doll. "Carrie?" she muttered, eyes closed. "Why do you think Dog stopped bothering you?"

"Because he wised up."

"No. Because Delmar closed in on him behind the Blue Crab one night and beat the daylights out of him. I watched. Delmar has never been so mad before or since. And Delmar doesn't generally get mad. I told Dog that night that if he didn't leave you alone, I personally would cut off his privates with the meat slicer at the View 'n' Chew—and he knew I would."

"Why didn't you ever tell me this before?"

"You are such an idiot!" Earlene said, and sighed deeply. "You would have gone and told everyone, and more scandal this family did not need. Enough people thought Delmar and I *had* to get married!"

"Earlene, I never knew. You and Delmar did that for me?"

"Well, who was going to do it? Wayne? Momma? I'm your big sister, Carrie."

Then, with a small sigh, my sister passed into the sleep of the totally depleted.

I sat there and just looked at her, my mouth hanging open, seeing my sister in a whole new way.

13

It *Is* As Bad As You Think
and They *Are* Out to Get You

Early the next morning, the beach at Rehobeth was almost deserted. I'd found a place to park nearly in front of Au Temps Perdu, my favorite clients' shop. Since I had an hour to kill before they opened, I grabbed a cup of coffee for my hangover and took a long stroll up the sand, letting the ocean lick at my bare feet.

The only other people up and about were surf fishermen and a couple of little kids with a kite. Over the roar of the surf I heard only the happy screams of children mingling with the keening of the gulls.

I set my sights on the distant point of Poodle Beach and inhaled the familiar comforting smell of the sea.

When we were kids, before Wayne went away, our family would rent a house at the beach every year. Somewhere, there were pictures of us when we were young, lined up in our wet, sandy bathing suits, squinting into the sun. Even Momma and Daddy were young back then, him looking bony in his baggy bathing trunks and Momma spilling out of her tight white bathing suit.

As a high wave rolled across my legs, I gasped with the shock of cold and wished I felt better about myself in a bathing suit.

"Look at you! You can't fit into anything!" Momma hissed, and I was suddenly ten again, standing in the dressing room at the Pink and Blue Shoppe on the boardwalk while she jerked and pulled at the dress she had selected for me. *"You're just too fat to wear anything pretty! We'll have to take you to the Chubbette department!"*

The anger and disappointment she expressed could have been a whip, the way her words stung me as she turned me this way and that in front of the unforgiving mirrors so I could see the way the bright plaid stretched across my stomach and chest. *"Look at that! Why can't you be pretty like Earlene? I never have any trouble finding her clothes!"*

Tears welled up in my eyes and I felt humiliated and rejected. *"I'm sorry, I'm sorry,"* I sobbed as she yanked the dress over my head and stomped out of the dressing room in disgust, pulling the skimpy green curtain behind her like a farewell. Tearfully, I pulled on my own clothes, too ashamed to come out of the dressing room as I heard her bitterly tell the clucking saleslady, *"I don't know what I'm going to do with that one! This is a size fourteen and she can't get into it!"*

"Bite me, bitch," I said, snapping out of my bitter reverie. "I'm alive and you're dead."

There was no one to hear me beneath the roar of the surf, and certainly no one to see the hot tears stinging my eyes behind my shades.

Maybe it wasn't so bad that she was dead and I survived. I sat down on a wooden jetty and gazed out to sea. It seemed to me as if every happy memory of my childhood was tainted by something nasty my mother had done.

No wonder Wayne had been so happy to get out of the house, when they'd offered him all those scholarships. Wayne, the genius, should have been the lucky one. But he wasn't. The family curse followed him all the way out to Los Alamos . . .

The family curse. Great way to think of your own mother. Momma having conjugal visits at the prison. Even dead, she was trouble.

To my great joy, Alonzo had been gone when I woke up, and so was Earlene, who must have crawled off the glider at some point in the wee hours and gone on home. In the hot bright light of day, I really didn't want to think about last night.

I stared out across the water and sipped at my coffee. Far, far out, a school of dolphins rose and fell in the water, joyously dancing northward. I envied them their freedom.

I was in a much better mood when I walked into Au Temps Perdu. The familiar, heady whiff of sandalwood greeted me before I was even in the door, and a bliss of objets d'art met my eye.

You've got your low-enders and your high-enders. These clients were definitely the highest of my high-enders. Oh, I have people who sell a much more expensive grade of stuff, but they lack the style. And style is everything in this business, especially in a resort town.

Taken out of its setting, perhaps that Depression glass sitting on those wooden milk crates wouldn't shine as it did here in this magic store. Taken away from its backdrop of '40s floral chintz, that battered tin breadbox would have looked prosaic and dull. Ari and Rick's great genius was in arranging things, making stuff like that ironstone pitcher look so wonderful and desirable that you knew you would carry that magic home with you. Suddenly, your house would look as bright and airy and charming as Au Temps, if you had those cleverly placed papier-mâché jack-o'-lanterns from the '50s. Your life would be gay and glamorous and exciting—your friends, amusing and witty—if you just owned that yellow-painted mule chest. Their great talent was to take ordinary, even useless, stuff and by placing it just so, make it desirable and brilliant and rare, so precious that it made you believe that stuff could transform your life.

Of course, when you got home, that pitcher might be just an old ironstone piece of no special character. The jack-o'-lantern for which you laid out a small fortune could turn out to be a dust collector. That painted pine chest, when standing in your living room, would look just like an old chipped and peeling thing that had stood in someone's barn for years, a home to mice and shadows.

Like the enchanted kingdom under the hill, viewed through a dreaming mind, when you awoke, it could be all smoke and mirrors, dry leaves and dust.

"Fairy gold," Rick once said, not without irony. "We sell fairy gold."

On the other hand, a purchase could transform your life. Something from Au Temps could make you handsome and popular, rich and fulfilled. It could bring back your hair and your dog and your ex. Get you elected president or made queen. I guess it all depends on whether or not you believe in fairy gold.

"Good morning—darling girl! Where the *hell* have you been?" Rick's dark head emerged from behind a rack of quilts and I was embraced in a sandalwood-scented hug that was deeply comforting. It's nice when someone loves you unconditionally, even if you are a little crazy.

"I've been out scouring the Eastern Seaboard looking for great things for Temps!" I gasped for breath. "Hither and yon, through a Disneyland of the mind, searching out the very best just for Au Temps's discriminating clientele."

"Bullshit," Rick said with a grin. "Ari will be so thrilled to see you! He's upstairs making phone calls. We're gearing up for the little season, when the big spenders come through town. None of this pre–Labor Day tire-kicker, trailer-trash stuff for the fall people—"

"You have to come out to the van and see what I have! Vintage embroidered table linens and an original *Star Trek* lunch box in almost mint condition, some great sixties paisley textiles, ironstone—all kinds of great stuff that I know you guys are gonna love!"

"One thing I love about you, Carrie. You're in touch with your inner homosexual."

I was pulling him out of the store, I was so excited. It's really nice to deal with people whose eye for stuff is sophisticated. They really appreciate the esoterics of this business.

I guess Ari heard me, because he came running down the stairs, his Birkenstocks clattering on the wood. The guys live in this glorious apartment above the store where all the really, really good stuff also dwells.

"What do we have here?" I was swept into Ari's enthusiastic embrace. Slightly older than Rick, he, too, smelled wonderfully of sandalwood and old books. As he lifted me off the floor in a bear hug, all I could do was giggle helplessly. Ari used to be a pro wrestler under the nom-de-turnbuckle "The Beantown Bruin," because he's as big as a bear and talks in a broad Back Bay accent.

"Come see, come see!" I squeaked. "I can't wait for you guys to see what I got for you."

"*Star Trek* lunch box, Ari," Rick said.

"Have you seen any of those fifties print tablecloths anywhere? We can't keep them on the shelves." Ari looked at me closely. "Something's wrong, isn't it? You look just a teeny bit beat, Carrie."

Trust Ari not to miss a trick. That might have been the secret of his success on the canvas. The pair of them gazed at me with all the sympathy of two gay men who always look their best.

"Well, my mother just died, and I was up all last night with my sister," I admitted.

"Oh, dear girl! What a dreadful thing!" Rick clucked sympathetically. "When my mother died, I was a wreck for months. There's just something about death that brings out the worst in everyone, isn't there? Is she being a beast, that sister of yours?"

Thinking about last night's events, I had to laugh, which may not have been appropriate for someone in deep mourning. "You don't know the half of it," I said quickly. "Come see all the stuff I brought you, then you can make me one of your cappuccinos and I can tell you all about it. I think you are the only people I know who could appreciate the whole horrible mess. I mean, you've met my family."

As I spoke, I was dragging them out to the curb. When you have great stuff, you really want to show it off. But when I started pulling treasures from the clutter of the front seat to their appreciative ooh's and ahh's, I found I couldn't wait to regale them with the story of my mother's fall from grace, not to mention that alligator pit.

"Your mother led an exciting life."

"Having met her a time or two, I would think she would love the idea that she was eaten by alligators," Ari observed dryly. "It's so dramatic, yet full of postmodern irony."

"Miss Audrey was totally postmodern, in her own way," Rick mused sadly. "She will be missed."

"I found some truly fabulous stuff recently," I said as I walked around the van and unlocked the back doors of my vehicle, "and I've been saving the best for you guys. Believe me, I wouldn't even let Jean over to Fenwick get even a hint that I had this stuff—"

With a grand gesture, I threw open the doors.

And the three of us gasped at the sight of a disheveled Alonzo Deaver sitting on the futon, munching a Snickers bar.

"Howdy!" he exclaimed happily, not looking the least bit flustered.

"Look, Ari"—Rick leaned against his companion—"she's brought us a man!"

"Is he collectible?" Ari rubbed his beard.

"Only if you're the law," I replied.

Alonzo took another complacent bite of his Snickers.

14

Another Long Sad Story

"When I die, if I go to hell, I'm gonna be okay. You know why? I'm gonna get a job assigning people their punishments. And the ones who piss me off are going to get the most creative eternity anybody ever saw. Forced to watch syrupy old Doris Day movies forever. Waiting in the bus station in Wilmington, Delaware, for a bus that *never* comes." I was fuming, pedal to the metal, hurtling the van through Shaft Ox Corner with a fine case of road rage. "And I'm gonna start with those two. You'd think they'd be thrilled to take you off my hands. Hide you in the gay community somewhere. But noooo. Some people are just too law-abiding for their own damn good."

"Weeeeelll, it wasn't really my fault." Alonzo took a big bite of his burger. "I was out and about this morning early, and I seen this guy comin' up the road toward the house, so I ducked into the van. It was the closest hidey-hole I could find."

I cursed myself for not checking the back before I took off this morning. But why would I even think of doing that? Shit.

If I had, the town criminal would have been someone else's problem by now.

Yes, I was still stuck with Alonzo. What was really ticking me off was that he had absolutely no plans for his future on the lam. As unconcerned as a ten-year-old, he was happily chowing down on the last of the Mickey D meal I'd purchased for him on our way out of Rehobeth. I'd never seen anyone eat four Quarter Pounders in one sitting before, but I have a strong feeling prison food isn't all that *delicioso*. Although, the way things were going, I realized I might find out firsthand.

"Can't I drive you up to Harrington or somewhere and put you on a bus? Don't you have relatives or friends somewhere who will help you start a new life?"

"Nope." Alonzo munched happily. "My folks are all dead or disowned. Anyway, while I was in jail, I read this book that says the Chinese think if you save someone's life, you're responsible for them forever."

"But *I* didn't save your life, Alonzo." I gritted my teeth. I really should have just dumped him out right there, in the middle of Slower Delaware. I mean Shaft Ox Corner is halfway between Gumboro and the beach. If I'd let him out there, he would have coped just fine. Nobody looks for anybody in Gumboro, Delaware.

"Look at me as a legacy." He stuffed some fries into his mouth. He was really enjoying that Mickey D; he was making smacking noises. "I mean, you inherited me from Miss Audrey. She got me to break out of jail. She was gonna help me escape. So you kinda inherited me, like a debt."

"Like a *bad* debt. Just what did you and Momma have in mind, once you busted out of the big house?"

"Well, she thought I should go to Florida. She said I could get some fake ID's and get a new life and a new job. She thought it was just terrible that I was in jail in the first place. Poor Miss Audrey. I can't believe she's gone."

What I couldn't believe was that she was boinking him in the jail's conjugal trailer. Well, actually, I could; I just didn't want to. To drive the image out of my head, I quickly asked, "Remind me Alonzo, what were you in jail for?"

"Weeeeell"—Alonzo stretched out the word as far as he

could—"it really wasn't my fault. Not really. It's not like I planned it or anything. It just sort of, you know, happened. It had to do with a gun."

Then it came back to me, the story Desiree had told me about the raffle. Still, I thought it would be fun to hear it from Alonzo's point of view. So I said nothing, just waited for him to continue.

"Weeeell, see, the Conservative Christians Central Committee held this gun raffle to support teaching gun safety in the schools. I mean, after that kid down to the high school shot up alla them people, I guess they figured if he woulda had some firearms training, he wouldn't've missed. They do love the Second Amendment, those ones."

"Doesn't that sound just like those redneck idiots? Raffle off a handgun because a kid shot up the local high school? They don't have enough sense to pour piss out of a boot, that bunch. They're too dumb to be allowed around firearms."

Alonzo missed my sarcasm entirely. My indignation flew right over his poor head. "It wasn't no long gun. It was this really nice .44 Mag. All silver and nice. A real fine piece." He sighed wistfully.

"Isn't that a tasteful thing to raffle off, a handgun."

"Oh, she was pretty. And the chances were only a dollar apiece. I just won a hundred bucks in the lottery, so I figured, easy come, easy go, right? Well, I musta been on a winning streak that week, because when I went over to Omar's store, they told me I'd drawn the winning ticket. Man, I never win anything, so I was really happy."

His breath was sweet with McDonald's secret sauce. He took a deep breath. "So I went on into the Conservative Christians HQ to collect my gun. It wasn't much of a headquarters, either, just some old storefront over in town in an empty strip mall. But all these fine, important Devanau County people were there to congratulate me, all these women done up with big old hairdos, and men in suits. And people from the paper come to take my picture. So they had this ceremony, and they gave all these speeches about Jesus loving the armed and dangerous, and about the Godless Liberal Media eroding our public schools 'cause they don't like prayer, and how old white guys rule. It was all pretty hinky, so I just wanted to get my gun and get out of there. I figured I could sell it for a couple, three hundred bucks. So, everything was goin' just fine until Sheriff Briscoe and Deputy Johnny Ray Insley came in late, and Briscoe looks at me and says, 'You can't give this man a firearm, he's a convicted felon,' by which I guess he meant that time I stole that Ford tractor, which I did, but I was drunk, so it shouldn't have counted."

He drew a deep breath. "Then, there was some coming to Jesus about this, that, and the other thing, and they were all getting mad because the reporters were there taking pictures and writing all this down for the newspaper and the TV, and I guess the Conservative Christians Committee was getting pretty upset, so they tried to take that .44 Mag out of my hands, after they'd already given it to me, and made me stand there for about twenty years of windbag speeches. So, when one blue-haired old lady with a lotta diamonds called me some nasty names and tried to snatch that gun out of my hand after I won it fair, I guess I sort of lost it."

"What did you do?"

"Wellllll, I guess I sort of turned that gun around and held it on all them people and told them to give me their money and their jewelry. You have to understand that I really did get mad. I never did like to be called names, even when I was a little kid. Stuff like that hurts, you know?"

"I know," I said, struggling to keep a straight face.

"So I cleared 'em all off of their money and stuff, and I moved on out of there as fast as I could. I was mad as fire, Carrie, I surely was. Then that woman called me common sorry white trash."

By then, I was laughing so hard I had to pull off Route 54, right on the shoulder by the pig farm. "I'm sorry, I'm sorry, Alonzo, but the image of you holding up those fools with their own gun is just priceless. I would have paid money to see that! And they deserved it, too. That old blue-haired lady had no right to call you common sorry white trash!" Okay, so that's what he was, but she had still no right.

Alonzo allowed himself a small grin. "That's what I told myself when I pawned all the jewelry and stuff. Went up and played the slots at Dover Downs. I had a fine old time, I did. Played the one-armed bandits 'til all the money was gone, then come back and turned myself in."

"I must have been way out of town for this. I never even heard about it."

"Well, it was a nine-day-wonder there for a while," Alonzo admitted with some satisfaction. "Anyway, Judge Fish didn't think it was all that funny and he's a Democrat. I got five years for it, and would have done three, suspended for good behavior, if Miss Audrey hadn't gotten involved."

"How was that?

"Welllll, she was takin' this political science course or something over to the college, and she got all pumped up and had this notion that I was this po-litical prisoner, that I had done this great po-litical act in showing up the Gun Nuts—that's what she called the Conservative Christians, the Gun Nuts. And that's when she started visiting me. Hell, I ain't po-litical. I never voted in my life but once, and that was when Omar paid me twenty-five dollars to vote for him on town council, which was a waste, because I wasn't registered to vote. Miss Audrey said I was like this South American guy, Hey Guava or something, that I was a hero."

"You mean Che Guevara?"

"That's it. Hell, I ain't no hero, I'm just a small-time crook. Everybody knows that. But when Miss Audrey had an idea in her head, well, you really couldn't shake her of it."

I had to agree with that.

"So that's why she wanted to bust you out, right?"

"That's exactly it. Because she thought I was like that Hey Guava guy."

I put my head down on the steering wheel.

"Oh, Momma, just wait 'til I get my job in hell."

There's not much landscape on the inside of the Delmarva Peninsula. A hamlet here and there where the Stardust Beauty Salon or a fruit stand is the main business, vast yellow fields of soybeans and corn to feed the endless chicken houses, a woodlot here and there along the flat twisty two-lane blacktop, a smattering of houses, everything baking in the white-hot sun.

"You know, Earlene's boys go to the community college. They probably have about eight or ten fake ID's apiece," I told Alonzo. "I bet they know someone who could set you up with a whole new set of papers. I could give you a hundred dollars and bus fare and you could go to Florida and start a new life. Wayne's down there."

"Maybe," Alonzo agreed. I guess he was so used to other people making decisions for him that he couldn't make them for himself. Jail could probably do that to you.

"Say, how *is* Wayne?" he asked. "I haven't seen him since we were in Oysterback Middle. We was best buds when we was kids. We used to swim together off the old bridge."

"I remember that. There was a whole bunch of us kids who used to jump off those pilings. You, me, Wayne, Barbara Reisert, Dina Wilner, Huddie Swann, Susan Anderson, Junie Red-

mond. I remember how cold the water was in the creek, even on
the hottest summer day. Even Earlene used to come up there
when it was real hot." I smiled in spite of myself. "Boy, that
seems like a long time ago, when we were really little."

"Wayne made a raft out of those old inner tubes, and we
floated all the way to Cedar Point. Then we had to paddle home
against the current. So he figured out a way to attach a sail to
the tube raft. Wayne was always really smart."

"Yeah, I remember Wayne used his own bedsheet. Momma
was furious, but Daddy laughed and laughed. I guess that's
when they started to realize Wayne wasn't like other people."

"He sure wasn't. Wayne could always figure out some invention or something. And he was way ahead of the rest of us in
class. Miz Weston said he was a genius."

"Turned out she was right. When he was in the ninth grade,
the school district sent him up to Baltimore to take all these
tests. It turned out he had an IQ that was so high it was off the
charts."

"Ah." The way Alonzo said it, it was like a sigh.

"Yeah. So they came and told Momma and Daddy that he
was really special, and he ought to attend this special school in
Baltimore for genius kids. And that was, like, the end of him."

"You said he was in Florida, so they didn't kill him."

I frowned out at the road. Far ahead of us, a mirage of sim-
mering water lay on the blacktop, disappearing as we
approached. "They might as well have. I mean, Wayne was
always really intelligent, we knew that. But they took him
away from the family, from Oysterback, from his friends, and
they made him into this Mozart prodigy genius robot kid. The
genius school pounded everything that was my brother out of
him." I fumbled for words, trying to explain something I'd
never thought about before. Probably because it was too
painful.

"I mean, it was like they made a little old man out of a normal kid. Not that Wayne was ever normal, but he was a kid, and he liked kid stuff like the Three Stooges and the Orioles—and swimming off the bridge with the other kids. And then, whatever they did up there, they took away his kidhood. When he came home at Christmas, he was like a gray little old man. A *cranky* little old man. It was as if they'd squashed everything that was Wayne out of him and replaced him with this unhappy genius kid who could do logarithms and split an atom but couldn't sit on the back porch and catch fireflies in a jar without giving us a lecture on their mating habits. He knew everything, but he didn't know the beauty or the wonder of any of it. They blinded him with science."

"Jeez, that sounds worse than the reform school I went to."

"He was a genius, all right. He went on to graduate from MIT at sixteen, but he was so socially retarded, he couldn't even talk to a girl without stammering. Last time I saw him, he was living on hot dogs and Pepsi, Alonzo. On white bread with ketchup. The worst thing is, he had no sense of humor left. I don't think he ever laughed again after he left here. But it didn't matter because he was a goddam genius."

"This sounds like a science fiction book I read once in jail. They programmed this guy to be a superintelligent robot and he lost his humanity."

"That book must have been about Wayne. Of course, after he went away to college and then Daddy died, we didn't see much of him. Or hear much from him, either. It was like he thought we were too dumb to understand him, and maybe we were. He was too busy being supported by the government. They sent him to grad school on all these fellowships, and then when he got his Ph.D., they sent him to work somewhere out west like Los Alamos, where he did all this top secret work on bombs and stuff. After that, we almost never heard from him, and when we did, he couldn't tell us where he was or what he was doing because it was all classified. It got to be as if we'd never had a brother at all, as if it was just Earlene and me."

"That's too bad. It sounds like one of them TV shows about android mutant gene replicants. Except those are all girls in black leather."

"I guess all he did was work. I don't think he had any friends or any kind of a social life or anything, from what he said later."

"Hard, very hard."

"I don't know. It was just sort of like he'd died. He just gradually faded away. At first I missed him, and then, when he wasn't there, I sort of half forgot he existed. Momma tried to keep in touch with him, but he didn't want anything to do with her. Not that I blame him for that. She was the one who sent him off to be raised by strangers, after all. I often thought she did it so she could brag about her son the genius, but now I wonder. Since she died, I'm not too sure about anything, including Wayne," I said, sounding as if I'd just come from Understatements "R" Us.

"Death does upset the apple cart. Poor Miss Audrey." Alonzo sighed mournfully. "I just can't believe she fell into that gator pit."

"Well, that's not the worst of it. A few years ago, Wayne finally had a long-overdue nervous breakdown. I mean, a complete break from reality. So the Los Alamos people put him in a hospital in New Orleans for a while, and then they turned him loose with a nice pension. He's okay as long as he takes his meds, but Wayne doesn't always remember to drop a chill pill, and then he gets into trouble. It's kinda like he's there, but he's not really there. He drifted around for a while, then he ended up in Florida. He says that's the last place the aliens will land, or something. He hates science. You can't bring it up around him or he has a fit. But all of a sudden, he had all this time on his hands, so he's started to experiment. Like having a delayed adolescence. He's tried a little bit of everything, including drugs I never heard of. So far, he's joined a cult, lived under a railroad bridge, announced he is Elvis reincarnated, illustrated an underground comic book, and worked as a produce clerk at the Trading Post. And it was that last that really got to Momma. She thought being a supermarket clerk was below his abilities. Like wearing a peach-colored robe and dancing around airports was some kind of lateral move from being a nuclear scientist. Happily, he'd moved down to the Keys to do all of this, and no one there seems to think he's too odd or a danger to others. From what I can tell, he's finally found a place where he fits in. But Momma really had trouble with the idea that he was down there spraying lettuce and radishes, so she rushed down there to straighten him out. And that's when she fell into the alligator pit at Gator Gardens."

"A terrible, terrible thing," Alonzo agreed solemnly. I didn't know whether he was talking about Wayne's job or Momma's demise. I didn't ask; I just drove.

We were both silent for a while, contemplating the strange train they call life.

On the east side of 113, we stopped at a gas station and bought sodas from the machine. As we sat on the curb, stretching our legs in the shade of a pin oak, allowing the icy Mountain Dew to slip down our parched throats, I was amused to note that no one paid the slightest attention to the most wanted man on the Eastern Shore. Maybe because everyone in Slower Delaware looks as if they are wanted somewhere other than here.

But it did occur to me that if Alonzo was going to wander about locally—and it appeared this was the plan—I needed help in the worst possible way.

15

So I Quit the Police Department And Got Myself a Steady Job

The View 'n' Chew is Earlene's natural habitat, the place where she is queen of all she surveys. Her queendom is on Log Cabin Lane, between Patti's Christian School of Tap and Ballet and the post office. Fortunately, at this late hour, both were closed.

The View 'n' Chew always smells wonderfully of olive oil and cheese steaks. True to Earlene and Delmar's code of ethics, the place is so clean, you could eat off the floors, and the only thing dirty is the X-rated video collection hidden away in the back closet.

Earlene was cutting paper-thin slices of ham on the meat slicer when I fell through the door, gasping for breath. And the way she was pushing that piece of meat through that blade didn't make me feel all that sanguine about the news I was about to deliver.

Neither did the fact that Deputy Johnny Ray Insley was browsing the new videos and waiting for her to build his lunch. What Johnny Ray lacks in smarts, he makes up for in sheer arrogance. He is proud of saying that the Marines made a man out of him, which I'm sure makes us all relieved. The Marines have their failures like the rest of us. He is certainly Sheriff

Briscoe's least competent deputy. And, of course, he's from Oysterback, so we all know what he's like.

Behind his back, I was making crazy faces at Earlene and
waving my arms around. Even after all those years of playing
charades, I still couldn't figure out how to pantomime *Help!*
Alonzo Deaver is in the van!

Earlene must have gotten the idea that something was
wrong, though. Until that moment. I'd never known what it
meant by saying that someone turned as white as a sheet.

Johnny Ray, ever alert, turned and saw me. He squinted
behind his Ray•Bans and bobbed his shaved head. "Hey there,
Carrie. I was just about to call you. Like I was just tellin' Earlene, there's an ex-caped convict on the loose, and he's been
spotted around here." As usual, he was full of the self-impor-
tance of the not-very-bright-with-a-little-authority. I heard
when he first went on the force, he told everyone he couldn't
wait to shoot somebody. See what I mean?

Earlene mugged at me behind his back. She had more
expressions than a set of Noh masks, but I didn't need any
coaching to play ignorant.

"Is that right?" I was all wide-eyed innocence, like a bad
actress in community theater. "Jeez. I heard something about
Alonzo Deaver being around, but I've been so involved with my
mom's funeral that I hadn't paid much attention."

Johnny Ray squinted at me behind his bad shades. "Well,
keep an eye out for him, because the info we got from the
prison says that your mother was in contact with 'im. So we
think he could be around here somewheres." He patted the gun
on his hip as if to make sure it was still there, sort of like a phal-
lic extension.

"I was just telling Johnny Ray that Momma was a good
Christian woman who took to heart St. Paul's command to visit
the sick and imprisoned," Earlene said stiffly. "Here's your

ham sub, Johnny Ray. That'll be five-fifty. I didn't charge you for the extra cheese."

Johnny Ray slapped an X-rated video on the counter. He pulled a toothpick from the cup and stuck it in his mouth. Slowly, he fumbled into his wallet for his cash and counted out a bunch of singles as if each one were made of solid gold.

I was edging toward the door, hoping I could head Alonzo off at the pass before Johnny Ray came out and saw him sitting in my van. Johnny Ray may not be the brightest bulb on the string, but even he could recognize an old Oysterback High classmate wanted by the law.

"You know, Alonzo always was a bad actor," Johnny Ray said. "Steal this, steal that. But that thing he pulled off with the Conservative Christians, that was a hangin' offense. He made a mockery of the Second Amendment. He made a mockery of our God-given right to bear firearms."

"I didn't know there was anything in the Bible about guns." It was out of my mouth before I could stop myself. I watched Earlene have a quick, silent fit behind the counter. It occurred to me that if she kept rolling her eyes back like that, they might stay that way.

"You don't fool around with guns," Johnny Ray said, all huffed up.

I didn't bring up the time he dropped his side arm in the Blue Crab and it went off and shot the Elvis-on-velvet painting in a very personal place, or the other time when this big drunk waterman took his .38 away from him in a brawl and shot out the windows of the post office. Or the time he ran the cruiser into the side of the church, or, well, the list went on. But no, I wasn't bringing any of it up. I was too busy edging toward the door, desperate to hide Alonzo, who was lounging in the passenger seat of my van.

Johnny Ray took a deep breath. "Not that I don't feel bad for

Miss Audrey, dying in Florida like that and all, but you got to watch out for a dangerous criminal like Alonzo—"

I was breaking out in a thin, sticky sweat. "I think I left the lights on and I'll run the battery down if I don't—"

Earlene is nothing if not quick on the uptake. "Johnny Ray, I think you've already seen *Boner IV*. You want *Boner V*." She waved the cassette box at him. My sister loathes the X-rated videos, but Delmar says they paid for their trip to Hawaii last year. If they weren't in a closet behind a beaded curtain you have to be eighteen to pull back, I don't think she would stand for having them at all, with her being so churchy and all, but her conscience seems to have a convenient dispensation for any sin that makes a buck.

"Have I?" Johnny Ray toddled on back to the closet and I made my getaway.

Alonzo wasn't in the passenger seat, although there was a big pile of fast-food wrappers where he had been. I quickly opened the back of the van, but the only contraband in there was a couple of Ferrus's decoys. I even checked the futon to make sure he wasn't hiding under the quilt.

I was standing there with my mouth hanging open when someone banged on the open doors behind me. I almost jumped out of my skin.

"You be careful, you hear?" Johnny Ray yelled at me. "He could be out here anywhere or he could be halfway to hell by now. So watch out!"

"I will." My voice was a croak.

I watched him until he got in the cruiser and drove away, off no doubt to a quick lunch and a quiet snooze behind the fence at the softball field. Johnny Ray has snoozing on the job down to a fine art. I don't know how he's managed to avoid being caught by Sheriff Briscoe all these years.

As soon as he turned the curve in Black Dog Road, I ran back in the store.

"Alonzo's back! I mean, he *was* back. He was in the van when I got to Rehobeth this morning, but I lost him in the parking lot!" I was out of breath. *Please, God,* I prayed, *get me out of this and I'll stop smoking and this time I mean it.*

As if God believes that.

"I mean, he's still around here!" I finished, leaning on the counter. "He was in the van, and then when I went out to warn him, he'd disappeared."

"I praise the day Dr. Wheedleton put me on Prozac." Earlene looked at me as if my head was what she wanted to put in the meat slicer next. "You took him to the beach and then brought him back? Carrie, what *were* you thinking?"

"I couldn't get rid of him! I tried, but he wouldn't go. He says that since Momma saved his life, there's this Chinese idea that you and I, as Momma's heirs, are responsible for him from now on!"

"I don't suppose it's too late to turn him in?" She looked out the window. "Maybe we should call Johnny Ray back."

"It would be fine with me. If we had Momma here, we'd have all three stooges in one place. What was she *thinking,* Early?"

"I know what I'm thinking right about now, and that's that if I had taken him all the way to Rehobeth Beach, I would have left him there to fend for himself. I thought he would be up and on his way this morning!"

"Well, I'm handing him over to you, Earlene, if he hasn't taken off for the marsh. In which case, he can go hang with the Boone brothers."

The Boone brothers.

We both shuddered at the thought.

16

Green City on a Marsh

"If he's taken off to the marsh, then he's probably gone to see Gabe and Mike Boone. And that means he's no longer our problem. No sane person ever goes near the Boones."

Earlene washed her hands and came out from behind the counter. She sank down in a booth and I slid in on the other side. In midafternoon, suspended between the lunch rush and the dinner hour, the View 'n' Chew was deserted and the red pleather upholstery was slippery and cool. How Earlene could work around hot, greasy grills and tubs of mayo all day and still look cool and pressed is beyond me, but she does it.

"No *sane* person. But I'm not entirely sure Alonzo is sane," I said. "He certainly lacks common sense."

"If common sense were a requirement for sanity, we'd all be up at the Towers Hospital in Cambridge." She put her feet up on my side and sighed with relief. "I will be so glad when Delmar gets back. He massages my feet, you know. Besides, this place just eats up your life when you have to run double shifts. Thank the Lord I got the boys to work tonight, as soon as they get in from school. I don't think I could stand one more person coming in here and talking about Momma. They're all acting so sympathetic, but you know they're dying for details. And then they get to talking about Alonzo and I want to scream. Until you came in, I was all ready to believe last night was a real bad dream. Or at the very least, that he'd gone on his way. Give me one of your cigarettes."

"I guess we should have said something to Johnny Ray, but when he made that crack about Momma, it was all I could do not to smack him upside his shaved head. Little Nazi." I pushed my cigarettes toward her, then leaned back in the seat and closed my eyes. I was exhausted and I knew she was too. Too tired to fight. "Maybe we should just call the sheriff. Wesley Briscoe's a nice man. He'll understand. He always reminded me of Daddy."

"I just don't want Momma's name dragged through the mud. Or ours, either. If it ever gets out that she was sleeping with Alonzo Deaver, for God's sake, we'll *never* live it down." She wiggled her toes out of her clogs.

"Well, if Johnny Ray knows, you can bet all of Devanau County knows. Let's just hope the prison people weren't all that forthcoming."

Earlene sighed, and rubbed the bridge of her nose between her thumb and forefinger. "Oh, Carrie. You just *know* they were. Alonzo is going to be all over the news. I'm just waiting for the TV news truck to drive up and that spray-headed blond reporter to poke a camera in my face."

"Oh, no, not that. I hadn't thought about the news. I wish Momma were alive again so I could kill her all over again. No, I don't. But we are so screwed, Early."

"Don't use that kind of language, and don't even think those thoughts. That's nasty." But her heart wasn't in reprimanding me. She knew what I said was pretty much what she was thinking too.

"Maybe you and I need to go on a trip. I understand Harpers Ferry is nice this time of year. I haven't been in Cumberland in a while. Who knows what I could pick up there, tons of unpicked stuff, I bet. Berkeley Springs is nice too. We could soak in the mineral baths, get massages, stay in a nice bed and breakfast 'til it all blows over. Maybe it's time to head for the hills."

For a minute, I thought I had her, but Earlene is Earlene, and being Earlene, will go down with the ship. "We still have to see Parsons Dreedle and talk to Reverend Briscoe about the funeral service. And Delmar and Wayne should be home soon. Delmar called last night. Wayne's bail hearing is definitely set for today. Maybe they'll let him out."

"Isn't bothering airport people a federal offense or something?"

"The last thing I want is Delmar to come home to this mess. His blood pressure is over the roof as it is, Carrie. He'll have a heart attack."

"Well, that's what comes from being a law-abiding citizen." I got up and made us each an iced tea, heavy on the Sweet'n Low and the lemon. In spite of the air-conditioning, I felt clammy. "I'm sorry, Earlene. I should show more respect for a man who beat the crap out of my would-be molester. I just wish I'd known earlier. You're right. This is not something Delmar needs to deal with. Or us, either."

"If anyone asks, we know nothing, nothing at all, right?" Earlene took a healthy slug of iced tea, jamming the straw in and out of the ice. "Are we clear on that?"

"Alonzo who?"

"Exactly."

We were grinning at each other when the phone rang.

I crawled over the counter and answered it, looking around for a pad and pencil to take an order. "View 'n' Chew."

"Earlene?"

"No, it's Carrie."

"Hi, Carrie. This is Desiree. I'm over at the Salon de Beauté, and I think we've got something that belongs to you two."

•

It's a ten-minute ride to Doreen's Curl Up 'n' Dye Salon de Beauté. Earlene did it in three and she laid a patch when she pulled up. She was practically out of the car before it stopped, and I was right behind her.

The smell of hairspray and apple-scented gel hit me like a pie in the face. And the sight of Doreen's latest hairdo, a medley of spikes and spit curls, tinged a screaming stop-sign yellow, sent me reeling backward. You'd never know the woman was a PTA mother of four and the loyal wife of Junior Redmond.

"You get Radio Hanoi on those?" I asked Desiree Grinch, whose head was covered in rollers.

"I'm getting my wig whacked and colored." Desiree grinned, flapping her black plastic smock at me as she spun around on her chair. "You didn't think that *I Love Lucy* red was real, did you?"

"Hi, Earlene! Carrie, honey, you really need to take care of those frizzies," Doreen greeted me, professional to the (split) end.

"Where is Alonzo?" Earlene yelped.

"Right here." Doreen spun a chair around and we were treated to the sight of Alonzo, head turbaned in a towel, his lanky body disguised beneath a smock. He was grinning like the fool I knew him to be.

"How did you get here?" Earlene put her hands on her hips, doubtless to keep herself from hauling off and whomping on him.

"I seen Johnny Ray comin', so I went around through the marsh. I was sneaking along out back when Doreen spotted me."

Oysterback's favorite hairdresser snapped her gum. "Well, I knew it was Alonzo, and I had to grab on to him before Johnny

Ray saw him." She shifted back and forth on her clogs, crossing her arms over her black tank top. Just the hint of a *gotcha* grin played around her lips and she winked at me.

"You *do* know he's an escaped convict, don't you?" Earlene was pinching the bridge of her nose again. She sank into a dryer chair, staring at Alonzo as if he were an X-rated video she'd just found in the Disney section.

"Well, of course we knew," Desiree put in. "That's all anybody ever talks about anymore! This is the most exciting thing to happen since Faraday Hicks's pacemaker was put in." I wasn't entirely sure she was kidding.

"I told them how nice you'd been to me since I come back." Alonzo beamed. "Doreen thought I was gonna eat out of her garbage cans instead of hiding behind them, so I had to explain to her that you'd fed me real well."

"You just *had* to drag us back into this, didn't you?" Earlene's tone was nasty, but she still lay there limp as an egg noodle, her eyes closed, as if she were afraid what she would see if she opened them.

Not that I blamed her, oh no.

Desiree began to massage Earlene's shoulders. "It's okay, hon, really. There was no one here but Doreen and me."

"Nope. I saw 'im and I sent Jeanne home. She was done with her last client anyway. Poor old Mrs. Twilley. She only has about three hairs left, but she comes in to get 'em shampooed and set every week."

Thinking about Hudson's honey-pie wife didn't make me feel much better. I could just see that sweet young thing running home to tell Huddie all about Alonzo, and the next thing you knew, we would have some kind of *real* trouble on our hands.

Like we didn't have enough already. A whole world of trouble.

"Do you have a plan?" I asked. "Because Earlene and I are stone-cold out of inventory on What To Do With Alonzo."

"Well, I gave him a makeover." At the Curl Up 'n' Dye, a Doreen makeover is the ultimate solution for everything, including world peace and overpopulation, so I wasn't too surprised.

But when she whipped that fluffy pink towel off Alonzo's head and revealed his new buzz cut, platinum 'do, his own mother wouldn't have recognized him even when she was sober.

"I'm gonna miss that cholo." He looked at himself this way and that in the mirror, and ran his hand over the brushy stubble. I noticed that Doreen had also given him a very nice manicure and glossed his nails with a clear polish. Judging by his glowing pink skin, it was a safe guess that he had also copped a mud masque facial while she was at it.

"Like his nails? That's Tony Soprano Nude. It's a new shade." Doreen admired her own handiwork.

"You look like Billy Idol's evil twin," Earlene observed, fanning herself with a copy of *People.*

"I do, don't I?" Alonzo smirked at his reflection. "One thing's for sure—I don't look like somebody anyone's lookin' for, do I?"

"Not unless you go to an Ocean City gay bar." Desiree began unwinding her enormous rollers. Her hair, freshly colored, was the tint of new bricks. She stood in front of Doreen's row of mirrors beside Alonzo, both of them preening and admiring themselves.

"I don't look *gay*, do I?" Alonzo demanded. "Not that there's anything wrong with it," he added quickly.

I was so glad they had *Seinfeld* reruns in prison.

"Don't you take that set apart, Desiree." Doreen lurched toward her, brandishing her brush. "You always mess it up." Quickly, she took over unspooling the rollers from Desiree's head.

"You two look like you're going to the prom." Doreen clacked her gum, a constant accessory in her endless campaign to stop smoking.

"And Carrie's drivin' the limo." Alonzo preened. I had to admit I never would have recognized him in his present state. But on the other hand, no one would *want* to recognize him with that hi-ho silver hair. "Quick, turn on the TV! It's time for *Oprah!*"

Doreen rolled her eyes as she unspooled Desiree's hair. Released from its constraints, it sprang, as it always does, into a thousand precise ringlets.

Alonzo flipped on the tube and hunkered down on a chair stacked with back issues of *Vogue*. He had the attention span of a newt. "Shush! We never miss an *Oprah* in the dayroom!"

"What are you doing, Doreen, distracting him 'til Johnny Ray gets here?" Earlene was whispering out of the side of her mouth, but it didn't matter, because Alonzo was so enraptured by Dr. Phil that he wouldn't have noticed if we hogtied him.

Doreen gave my sister an indignant look. "Of course not! Why, Earlene, I have known you all my life, and I am shamed that you would think I'd ever turn a homeboy over to the Man. I'm an Oysterback girl! We don't do things like that around here, at least not to one of our own."

"No, we're just *disguising* him a little." Desiree bent over and shook out her hair to give it some more volume, teetering on an impossibly high pair of stiletto mules and showing off a nicely compact butt encased in a pair of orange capri pants.

"Look, it's not like the fish cops are looking for him for tonging off sanctuary beds or something. This is serious."

"Well, it seems very disrespectful to Miss Audrey, turning him in." Desiree's tone was totally matter-of-fact. "Her last wish seems to have been that he get away from here and start a new life. She was really inspired by that whole handgun flap."

Earlene and I exchanged a look. I thought my sister was going to faint. It was true. We *were* the last to know about Momma and Alonzo.

In short, it *was* as bad as we thought it was and they *were* out to get us.

"I could have used a new .38 myself." Doreen picked up a strand of my hair and clucked at my split ends. "But if I would've had my pick, I'd take the shotgun. I've about worn the barrel thin as paper on my old Remington, and I have a perfectly usable Ladysmith under the counter. Not that I think anyone would want to hold up a salon de beauté, but some of my clients are a little too high-maintenance for their own good. Speaking of which, I don't know what you've been washing your hair in, Carrie, but it feels like the underside of a Brillo pad. You'd better let me give you a hot oil treatment and trim you up."

Before I could squawk, she had me bent backward over the sink and was shampooing my hair. It actually felt wonderful; having someone wash my hair always does. "Boy, are you tense! I can't even move your scalp around, Carrie!"

I knew better than to protest. I submitted when she rubbed that oil stuff into my scalp and plumped me into her station. She whirred on the dryer and started hair rehab. "Is this the same cut I gave you last time you were in town? It looks like you slept on it wet."

"I did."

"Well, don't do it anymore. You get permanent bed hair that way." I think she also added something about no guy wanting to date a woman with bed hair, but I wasn't sure because the hair dryer was blasting in my ear.

It was nice and calm and full of whirring white noise under the Conair 2000. Desiree's, Doreen's, and Earlene's voices were just a dim murmur, and every once in a while I'd hear Alonzo chuckle at Dr. Phil.

"*Stand still,*" *my mother would say as she tugged at my hair with a brush.* "*You've got so much curl, I don't know why you're always complaining about it. I would have killed to have hair like yours when I was a girl.*" *I was wriggling and whining because every time she dragged the brush through my hair, it pulled at my scalp and hurt like having pins stuck in my head. Rats. She called the tangles rats.*

"*You have a lot of rats today,*" *she'd say. As if I could help it that I had a snarl of frizzy curls. I hated my hair. I loathed it with a passion, because it wasn't straight and blond, like Earlene's. In those days, it was the Farrah Fawcett look that everyone wanted, those wings and loops, as if that would make us all look like America's sweetheart. I used to roll my hair on orange juice cans and sleep on them. I used to iron it, on an actual ironing board. I used to get Doreen to use Perma Relax on it. And no matter what I did, it still came out a mass of frizz. No doubt it was my Oysterback mixed blood showing up. About the time I dropped out of college, I gave it up and let it go with the flow. I was tired of living a life in service to hair. And now, ironically of course, that I was past my fifteen minutes of cute, frizzy hair was highly desirable. Go figure. In the end, Momma turned out to be right. I was glad to have it. I just wish I'd had a chance to tell her that before she went to Gator Gardens. Everybody needs to know when they're right, even Momma, who was convinced she was always right.*

The silence when Doreen turned the dryer off was louder than the noise. It snapped me back into the real world.

"I know, I know. I just keep thinking that if Carrie found some nice guy and settled down, she'd be so much happier." That was Earlene.

"—Jack comes to work and writes down all the stories everyone tells, especially the older people. Says he's writing a book." Desiree was perched on the edge of Earlene's chair, her face right next to my sister's ear.

"He's single and she's single, why not?"

They broke off and looked at me. Desiree at least had the grace to wink. Earlene just looked as if she stood on her word and wouldn't back down. Well, maybe it's better to be talked about than ignored, but the marriage-and-kids theme was old, old, *old.*

"I know all about Jack Shepherd." Doreen scraped my hair back with a comb and began to spritz it. "Gets a cut every three weeks. Has dry hair, but it's thick. You'd never know he's getting thin on top. He's a very nice guy. He moved his boat here a few years ago, and took it out on weekends, and it was sort of like he'd always lived here. He socialized a whole lot. Then he told everyone he didn't get tenure at the college, and he moved down here full-time."

"He says he's writing a book about us." Desiree examined her fingernails. "He talks to everyone and makes notes. I don't know how far he'll get with it, though. A lot of the older people don't want to talk to him. You know how people are around here about come-heres and foreigners. Suspicious. A lot of the old folks don't like that whole outlaws-on-the-marsh thing dredged up, even if the proceeds we get from the Mosquito Festival pays for the fire department and the ambulance."

"Good luck to him. I tried to write a book once." Snip went Doreen's scissors right next to my ear; I could feel the cold metal. "It's a lot harder than you might think, especially if you don't read too much. You have to use all these words, for one thing. After about five pages, I gave up. What with Junie and the kids and the business, I just didn't have the time to think."

"Imagine that! I never knew you tried to write a book!" Desiree picked at a cuticle. "I swear, Doreen, you are just a bundle of surprises."

"There's a lot about me no one knows." Doreen's tone was complacent. "I've got a whole secret life."

"Yeah, but yours is all derived from those romance novels. Not like Momma. She had some *real* secrets."

"Carrie!" Earlene warned. "Why didn't you all tell me this was going on with Momma?" She glared at Doreen and Desiree.

"We didn't want to worry you." Desiree touched Earlene's shoulder lightly. "You have enough on your mind. And we knew you wouldn't approve."

"Besides," Doreen added, "it's none of our business."

As if that ever stopped anyone in Oysterback before.

"Well, it seems like that cat is out of the bag, and has been for sometime, Early," I said. "There's not much left to cover up."

"Oh, Audrey was a good old gal. She had her ways, but who doesn't? I can't count the times she sat in this very chair and told me she felt as if she was nothing——"

"——without a man," I finished.

"But why *that* man, of all God's creatures?" Earlene tilted her head at Alonzo, who was finding his spirit and totally oblivious of us.

"Why not?" Desiree inclined her curls at him. "He's not the brightest bulb on the string, but he's presentable, in a Wal-Marty kind of way. Besides, he was a captive audience. She knew where he was, all the time. When she needed him, she just drove over there. Then, when she was done, she could pop him back in the box and go on with her life. It seems to me that it was a perfect arrangement. Sex in the box."

"I'll tell the world. Sometimes havin' a man underfoot twenty-four-seven is just about more than I can take. Not that I don't love Junie, because I do—he's the best husband and father anyone could ask for—but pickin' up his dirty socks from where he tosses them under the bed, and the way he makes this *sound* when he brushes his teeth, like he's strangling a walrus in there. And him asking me, 'Why did you buy Chelsea those purple shoes?' and saying, 'Honey, I wish you could make a crab cake like my mom's'—well, I could just about kill him sometimes. When he goes off deer huntin', I breathe a sigh of relief. Of course, a day or two later, I miss him like crazy, but still. You can see the advantage to having a man you need to see only once in a while, and that with a very specific purpose in mind. Earlene, stop havin' fits. Sex is a natural part of life, even for a woman over fifty."

"I should hope so, or we're all doomed to a lonely old menopause." Desiree was trying out all the lipstick samples on her hand, holding the tubes up to her face as she looked in the mirrors. "Earl Don and I get along better now that we're divorced than we ever did when we were married. And the nookie is fabulous!"

"Oh, yeah. I could understand what Momma liked about the arrangement. But why in God's name did she want to bust him out of jail?" I asked.

"Because she needed the drama, that's what I think." Desiree gave me a level look. "Miss Audrey just thrived on excitement. And let's face it, as she got older, there were fewer and fewer men around she hadn't—I mean, they weren't paying her the attention she was used to getting."

Doreen snorted but said nothing.

Earlene collapsed again. "Oh, lord, Momma was a drama queen and she loved her men after Daddy died, but this—it—him. Oh, Lord. What was she thinking?"

"She wasn't thinking with her head, that's for sure. What part of her she was thinking with, I don't want to contemplate." I squirmed. "If it had pants, she was interested."

"Sit still, Carrie. I don't want to cut your ear off. It wasn't the men, it was the excitement. She craved action and drama. She wanted to be the corpse at every funeral and the bride at every wedding, Miss Audrey did."

Earlene put her head in her hands, her shoulders sagging.

"Don't feel bad, Earlene. Everyone loved Miss Audrey." Desiree patted my sister's shoulder again. "Don't be too hard on her. She saw one last chance to have a little romance in her life and she took it."

"Why didn't I see what was happening? How could she have pulled this off under my very nose?" Earlene was wailing.

"Because she knew you would have had her committed, not that I would have blamed you." I twisted around to look at my sister, and Doreen clapped my head between her hands and turned me around again. *Snip, snip,* and my hair fell away, spilling down the plastic smock, falling in great frizzy chunks to the floor.

"Close your eyes, Carrie. I don't like the look on your face when I cut your hair. It gives me the whim-whams." I closed my eyes. "Now, now, we're going to work this out. We owe Miss Audrey that much, don't we, Des?"

"Damn right. And we owe Earlene and Carrie, too. It's the right thing to do. Besides, it could be fun. Maybe Miss Audrey was on to something here. I've never helped an escaped convict before. I've done a lot of stuff, but this will be a first." Desiree clapped her hands in delight. "It's just like the sixties all over again! Hot damn! We fought the law and we won!"

"Not yet." Earlene's tone was gloomy.

"After she sort of, you know, went after Professor Shepherd, and he wasn't, you know, interested, that's when she thought about Alonzo," Doreen whispered in my ear.

I sneaked a look at her in the mirror, and instead caught the slow flush creeping up my face. At least that question was answered. But what good did that do? It wasn't as if I thought

Jack was, I don't know, attractive or anything. Did I? Of course not, I reminded myself sternly. You are totally gun-shy about men, and you enjoy living the life of a nun.

"Close your eyes! You havin' a hot flash, hon?" Doreen asked me. "How old are you? I had a cousin who went into the change when she was still in her thirties. She took a sledge hammer to her computer. Later, when she got some HRT, she said it was the best thing she'd ever done in her life, whacking that computer into the next world."

"Doreen, you stand in here all day and hear all the gossip. Did Momma really go after Jack Shepherd?" I had to hear this one twice to believe it once.

"Oh, Carrie, it wasn't any big deal. Miss Audrey just flirted with him a little, that's all." She began to attack my hair with a comb. I felt something new emerging from my head. "Hold on, don't look yet. I'm gonna try something different on you, and I don't want you yelling at me to stick to the same old thing."

"As long as you don't give me a cholo or something." I considered what she'd just said. "Just flirted with him. Well, Momma flirted with everyone who possessed even a hint of testosterone." Why did that make me feel even worse? "It's like that old Oysterback joke: 'Son: I found a girl from up the road and guess what, she's a virgin! Father: How do we know she's good enough for us if she ain't good enough for her own people?'"

"That was funny the first fifty times I heard it, but I don't see how it applies here. Hold still, hon. The thing is, Omar thinks—"

"Omar! What does Omar know about this?" Earlene, with the ears of a cat, missed nothing, and what she heard must have upset her; I heard something that sounded like a chair overturning.

"Now, Early, don't have a fit," Desiree said, soothing her.

"Omar happened to come by for a trim, and he was here when we found Alonzo behind the trash cans."

"Well, he's acting mayor," Doreen pointed out. "Seeing as how Pink Bladderwack's been in that coma for three years and people keep reelecting him anyway."

"He can't help it if he hit his head on the overhang at the marina. What if he comes out of it and finds out he's been defeated? He'll be so hurt, Omar says it might kill his will to live."

"I might remind you that I am on the town council too," Desiree sniffed. "We do a lot of important work for this town."

"Like anyone could forget," Earlene muttered. "Oh, my God. If Omar knows, the whole town knows. Carrie and I will go to jail for sure."

"Well, just Omar and Ferrus and me," Desiree assured us. "Just the town officers."

"It's not too late to go to Berkeley Springs, Earlene. Mineral baths. Massages. Bed and breakfast places with a Victorian theme."

"You all wouldn't run away now, just when it's getting good!" Desiree was indignant. But then, Desiree knows no fear. If she'd fallen into the alligator pit at Gator Gardens, she would have wrestled the damn reptile into submission and called it a growth opportunity.

"You have to relax, Earlene. We're gonna get this all straightened out." Doreen sounded pretty confident.

"I don't want Delmar coming home to this mess. He's already had to spend two days trying to get Wayne straightened out down there in Miami. If he gets here tonight with Wayne and finds out his troubles aren't over, it'll kill him for sure. His blood pressure is already over the moon!"

"One thing's for sure: Oysterback can handle only one crisis at a time, and Wayne is a whole walking crisis on his best day."

Desiree is nothing if not frank. "But don't worry. We'll come up with a plan to get Alonzo settled down, even if he has to go live with the Boone brothers."

"Hey, I heard that!" Alonzo looked up. "And I ain't havin' any of Gabe and Mike Boone."

"Okay, you can open your eyes now." Doreen tapped me on the shoulder. I opened my eyes and looked at myself in the mirror.

Instead of a frizzy flyaway mess, my hair was cropped into a halo of curls. I was looking at a whole different person. Without that curtain of frizz to hide behind, I actually had a face. And it wasn't a bad face. In short, Doreen had worked a miracle.

Before I could say something, the door banged open.

"I'm here to save you all! Ain't nobody move!" Johnny Ray yelled, swinging his gun around wildly.

17

Because We Say So,
That's Why

"For God's sake, Johnny Ray, put that damn thing down." Desiree marched across the floor and grabbed his automatic by the barrel, snatching it out of his hands as if he were an annoying little kid with a water pistol. "You're gonna shoot somebody."

"Don't make me send you your letter, Johnny Ray." Doreen shook her shears at him. "If little Miss Buck was here, you would have brought on her angina, then who'd play the organ at Miss Audrey's funeral?"

"I got a call from Miss Carlotta Hackett that there was a suspicious-lookin' man hangin' around the Dumpster." Johnny Ray peered around at us. I guess it was hard for him to see indoors in his mirrored Ray•Bans. "I figured Alonzo was in here holding you all hostage. Say, who's that guy over in the corner, watchin' *Oprah?*"

Alonzo turned and looked at what passes for the Man. You could see his Adam's apple sliding up and down his throat.

"Don't you recognize Wayne when you see him? Has it been that long?" Earlene was a little shaky, but she was fast on her feet. Lying doesn't come easily to her, but by God, she was good at it. I've never been so proud of her in my life. "Wayne, do you remember Johnny Ray Insley?" my sister prodded the escaped convict.

Alonzo just swallowed.

Johnny Ray stared at him. I guess it's not every day he sees a guy with a bleached-blond brush cut watching *Oprah.* "Is that you, Wayne? Jeez, I hardly knew you!" Oysterback's finest hooted.

"I've changed," Alonzo croaked. I could see the sweat on his upper lip.

"I'll say," Johnny Ray bellowed. "You've gone all Florida on us. You look like one of them Jimmy Buffett Parrot Heads now. Who'da thought? Back in junior high school, you were such a nerd that I used to beat you up all the time! Remember the time I dunked you in the terlit in the boys' room? Hoo-haa, those were the good old days, right, bunk?"

Alonzo gave him a ghastly grin.

"May I remind you that my brother is in town for his dear mother's funeral?" Earlene's voice could have frozen jalapeños. She rose to her full Christian magnificence, towering over the short arm of the law. "Can't you see he's grief-stricken?"

That sure did wipe the idiot grin off Johnny Ray's face. "Oh, yeah. I'm sorry about that." He had the grace to look abashed in the solemn presence of death.

Desiree opened the chamber of his gun and expelled the bullets. "You know," she scolded, "Sheriff Briscoe doesn't like you to go around with a loaded gun after that last incident." She rattled the slugs in her cupped hand like dice. "This thing could stand to be cleaned, too. Look at the dust in there! Don't you have some FP-10 anywhere? I'd be ashamed if *my* gun looked like this."

He twitched. "Well, what with the ex-caped convict runnin' around and all, I thought . . ."

"Don't think, Johnny Ray." Doreen waved a hand at him. "Miss Carlotta saw Wayne out there. He took out the trash for me. Poor old thing, she's gettin' about half blind and mostly deaf." Never mind that the woman had the spying capability of a Russian microwave bug; that was Doreen's story and she was sticking to it.

"Well, she does call 911 about once a month about prowlers, and it always turns out to be a branch of that old pin oak scrapin' against the back bedroom window . . ."

"I know. Viola complains about it every time she comes in for her bikini wax. She's tried time and again to remind Miss Carlotta that it's just that branch again, but the poor thing *will* call the dispatch." Doreen shook her head. "It's a waste of man-power, sendin' someone out there, but it's a 911, so half the time Junie has to get out of bed and go over there. He is chief of the VFD, after all."

"Aw, she just needs a man, that's all," Johnny Ray said with a wink. "A widow lady like her . . ."

"And now that we've solved *that* mystery, you'd best scoot. I've got this whole family to get cut and curled for the funeral, and I'd still like to get home tonight." Doreen was unyielding as she pushed Johnny Ray toward the door. "If I see anything that even *looks* like Alonzo, I'll call you first, but I imagine he's halfway to hell and gone by now."

Desiree handed him his gun on the way out the door. I noticed that she'd tucked the bullets into her pocket, but we all knew Johnny Ray had plenty more at home.

The bells on the door jingled as Johnny Ray exited stage left.

"Momma used to say a man who liked to play with guns probably was compensating for a small personal firearm," Earlene observed in a shaky voice.

There were a few seconds of silence, then we all fell into hysterical laughter.

"Earlene, you are a marvel and a thing of beauty!" Doreen said, giving her a hug.

My sister looked a little pleased with herself as she smoothed her slacks over her thighs. "I did what I had to do. I didn't know lying was so *easy*."

"Well, we'd better do what *we* have to do. Johnny Ray may be a fool and a half, but Sheriff Wesley Briscoe isn't, and if he comes down here lookin' around, we're cooked." Desiree rattled the bullets in her pocket.

Earlene was as pale as death, but not as pale as Alonzo.

"You've got to decide what you want to do. You can't hang around the West Hundred, unless you want to go out and live on the marsh with Gabe and Mike Boone."

"I'd rather go back to jail than live on the marsh with them two," Alonzo said with a shudder.

"Well, that rumor about them chopping up Daniel Harbeson, salting him down, and using him for crab bait isn't true, if that makes any difference," Doreen pointed out. "Although I don't know if I buy that story about Danny discorporating and going back to Uranus."

"The Boone brothers are just a pair of old stoners left over from the sixties!" Desiree waved an impatient hand. "They just like everyone to stay away from them out there so they can tend to their marijuana patch and collect those jars of mosquitoes for that scientist over to Mosquito Control."

"I just don't want to live with anyone who eats road kill." Alonzo crossed his arms over his chest. "I'll do anything else, but I won't live with them Boones. Besides, I hate Deadheads."

"And you call yourself a hardened criminal." Earlene shook her head.

"Hey! They got serial killers an' rapists over to the prison who'd rather get the needle than live with them Boones!" Alonzo was just a tad defensive. "Prison food ain't Desiree's cookin', but damn if I want to eat raccoon roadside fricassee or some poor ole chicken what met an untimely end under a Chinaberry poultry truck on Route 13!"

"Agreed." Doreen nodded. "But we got to figure out what we're going to do with you. Maybe we could hold a bake sale or a car wash or somethin' and raise enough money to get you on your way to a new and, hopefully, crime-free lifestyle."

"Far away from here," Earlene added.

"You just wait 'til Miss Carlotta comes in for her frost and rinse. I'm gonna make sure her hair is purple for a month," Doreen muttered.

"She meant well, I'm sure." I turned this way and that, looking at my new short hair in the mirror. I didn't know I had cheekbones, or if I did, I had forgotten. And a forehead. I have a forehead. And a neck. And ears in which I could now wear some cool antique earrings I'd been meaning to sell. Until this minute, I didn't think I deserved them.

"Just like she meant well when she told me having your van parked in the driveway lowered property values in the neighborhood." Earlene frowned as she looked at me, then smiled. "That *is* a terrific haircut. You look great."

"Well, she told me you were stealing boxes of Momma's stuff out of the house." I turned to Doreen. "Do you really think it looks good? My head feels ten pounds lighter."

"It's a really good cut," Desiree informed me. "You look ten years younger and twenty pounds lighter." She positioned herself so that I could see her face but Earlene couldn't. "Don't ask Earlene about those boxes," she mouthed.

"Yeah," Alonzo chipped in, "you look real good, Carrie."

Doreen had moved over to the back window. "Can you believe it? That fool Johnny Ray is out there digging through the garbage cans. Like Alonzo's gonna hide in there, as hot as it is." She tapped on the window. "Don't you go scattering my trash all over the place, Johnny Ray! I won't have it! You pick that stuff up! If there ever was an escaped convict hiding in there, he'd be long gone by now!" She glared through the glass, arms crossed. "Honestly, that man was behind the door when they handed out the brains." She rapped smartly on the glass with her knuckles again. "Stop that! Stop that right now! You pick that stuff up and put it back in the cans! I mean *now*, Johnny Ray!"

"This is not working out the way I planned it," Alonzo muttered. I think the seriousness of his problem might have started to hit home. Johnny Ray wasn't the only one who was behind the door when the brains were handed out.

"Johnny Ray's gone," Doreen said, turning away from the window. "Come on, let's rock and roll."

Ferrus T. Buckett lives far down on the edge of Great Devanau Marsh, in a little yellow house. He and Acting Mayor Omar Hinton were rocking on the front porch when Doreen pulled her Grand Cherokee into the rutted oyster-shell lane, neatly working her way around the piles of rusted appliances, car parts, and burned-out oil barrels in the littered wonder of Ferrus's yard. Mr. Toad's Wild Ride has nothing on Doreen's driving, but Ferrus's junk is all for show for the tourists, who think it makes his "antique" decoys all that much more authentic. Besides, she only knocked over a couple of the oil drums Ferrus uses to char those "antiques."

The men had their heads inclined to one side, and as we piled out of the Jeep, we heard the high, distant wail of the Oysterback Volunteer Fire Department's siren. It sounded like a banshee in heat on the dismal, humid air.

"That's a backup call for Patamoke," Ferrus announced knowledgeably.

"Yup, there'll be an ambulance call any second," Omar agreed. "Probably an accident out on Route 50. Them tourists can't get to Ocean City fast enough, can they?"

"What that means is almost everybody's out on the call, so we can call this little town meeting to order without worryin' about any goddamned sunshine laws. We got the acting mayor settin' right here and both council people present, and some voters, so I declare this meeting officially open." Ferrus grinned, showing off his new teeth.

"So declared," said Desiree as she tripped into the house, the screen door creaking behind her.

Ferrus turned a can of Miller beer in his callused hands. "Well, howdy do, Alonzo! Long time no see."

Omar allowed himself to rock a cycle. "Ladies. Alonzo. It's nice to see you. I like the new look, Alonzo."

"Mr. Ferrus, Mr. Omar," Alonzo said agreeably.

You'd think none of them had a care in the world. Sometimes men just amaze the daylights out of me. They both listened impassively as Doreen described our situation. "And, as mayor and the other alderman, we think you ought to step in and help us," she finished. "Just like what I said on the phone."

"So, Alonzo, you broke yourself out of jail," Ferrus offered. He was working with some sandpaper on a decoy merganser head. He'd soon have that whole bird done, painted, and buried in his manure pile to age nicely before he gave it an aged patina in the barrels.

"Yessir, I did," Alonzo admitted. "And I guess I shouldn't have, but I listened to other people." He sank heavily onto the porch step.

"I see Miss Doreen has worked her magic on you," Omar offered. "Your own grandmother wouldn't know you with that bleached-blond hair, boy."

"Well, yessir," Alonzo nodded. He ran his hand over the top of his newly shorn head. "I sorta look like one of them rock stars."

"Yeah, you look like somethin', young man." Omar regarded him over his glasses.

Neither of them mentioned *my* new do, I noted with a slighted feeling. On the other hand, I wasn't a buzzed and bleached blonde.

Ferrus's old Lab wandered over, sniffed Alonzo, then laid its head on the escaped man's lap. Alonzo began to stroke its graying muzzle and the dog sighed happily.

"See? What did I tell you, O? Ain't no harm in the boy. Blackie don't go to evil people."

"Well, the only reason I'm getting involved at all is because of Audrey and the girls," Omar replied, looking at Earlene and me as if we had somehow caused this mess, which maybe, in some roundabout way, we had. "We're family, after all."

"And you're acting mayor, so either you're in or out." Ferrus blew dust from his merganser head.

The VFD siren started up again, one long blast, and Omar squinted over the marsh at the town, distant and misty in the haze. "One good thing—almost every able-bodied man and woman in town will be at the accident, instead of mindin' the business at hand for us. That was the ambulance call, and they'll probably take out the meat wagon, too."

"Where's your scanner?" Doreen asked. She sank down in the old swing and patted the broken cushion for Earlene, who joined her.

"Don't need no stinkin' scanner, me," Ferrus said. "I just *sense* these things."

"That he does," Omar agreed. "Always has, ever since I was a boy. Damnedest thing you ever saw."

"You don't get to be the world's oldest waterman by bein' stupid," Ferrus said matter-of-factly. "I'm the seventh son of a seventh son and born with a caul."

"It's true," Omar said, nodding. "We was down the Bay one time, Ferrus, your daddy, and some others of us, fishing for drum, brightest, clearest day you ever saw, and we was pullin' in some big reds. Ferrus sniffs at the air and says, 'We'd best beat it back to land, boys. I smell a bad squall comin' up.' Well, some of the younger boys, and I was one of them in those days, laughed, but Ferrus fussed so that we gave in and beat it into Shellpile with that squall so hard on us, we could see the sheets of water and the waves following on our stern. Come up out of nowhere, waves as tall as I am and rain lashing us so hard we couldn't see a hand before our faces. If we hadn't beat it when we did, we might have been fish food ourselves. That was some blow." He nodded solemnly. "I never been so glad to see land in my life, before or since."

"We have no reason to disbelieve you," Doreen said. "That's why we're here. We got a problem. A de-lick-ate problem."

"And taking care of it is the last, decent thing we can do for Miss Audrey." Desiree appeared from within Ferrus's house and handed out ice-cold cans of Miller. It tasted really good in the heat. Desiree is one of those people who make themselves right at home. "And of course, Earlene and Carrie." She sat down on the steps beside Alonzo, and we all stared out across the marsh for a moment. From out here on Ferrus's neck, it looked as quaint and charming as a tourist painting, tiny houses nestled among old trees.

The high scream of the ambulance siren rose, then trailed away as it headed over the bridge, across the marsh, and into the mainland.

"Well, boy, what do you want to do?" Ferrus asked Alonzo.

We all turned to look at him.

"Well, I dunno. Sometimes I wish I'd never let Miss Audrey talk me into breakin' out. At least it was predictable in jail. But now that I'm out, I guess she'd want me to go on and maybe get a life somewhere. Go straight, get a job. Someplace warm. Winter's getting hard on me. Out here, everyone's crazy."

"We could send him back to Florida with Wayne," I told Earlene.

"That's a match made in heaven," she replied, but I couldn't tell if she was serious or not. She was, I noticed, actually drinking a beer.

"We still have to stash him 'til after the funeral. And with Johnny Ray and every good ole boy with an itchy trigger finger in town looking for him, stashing him is not going to be easy."

"There's the Boone brothers—"

"No!" everyone said at once.

An osprey circled overhead, then stooped over the gut, rising triumphant, a struggling fish in his talons.

"Thelma would never let me stash him at our house," Omar brooded. "My wife is a wonderful woman, but she has her limits. She doesn't even much like the grandkids staying more than a week."

"I've got the boys." Earlene sighed. "They're at the age when they don't notice much, but they probably would notice Alonzo."

"I've got Junie and four kids," Doreen noted. "Junie wouldn't hold with an escaped convict, though. I mean, that little thing about huntin' over bait went on the stet docket, but still . . ."

"Earl Don comes and goes. And I've got more drop-in company in my place than a public library. If you run an eating and drinking establishment and they can't find you in the Blue Crab, they think nothing of coming around back to the house, even the delivery men. I was in the shower the other day when the beer delivery came and he walked right into the bathroom to get me to sign."

"Well, there's Momma's house, but Jack Shepherd comes over and sleeps on the daybed in the Florida room."

I saw everyone looking at me as if a string of lights had suddenly gone on. "Oh, no." I started shaking my head. "Oh, no."

"Professor Shepherd! Damn, why didn't *I* think about him?" Ferrus chuckled, looking at me with a wink. "With that pretty new haircut, you could talk 'im into anything."

"Johnny Ray already thinks he's Wayne. Why can't we just leave it at that? Sort of like *The Purloined Letter*, that Poe story where something gets hidden in plain sight?"

"Because enough people around here *know* Alonzo," Desiree pointed out. "He's sort of famous in these parts."

"Hey, I'm a celebrity?" Alonzo glowed.

"Yeah, but you're famous for all the wrong reasons. Stealing bait, stealing live boxes, engine parts, crab pots, shrubbery——"

"Hey, *I* didn't steal them boxwoods from Shallow Shores Doublewide Park! That was someone else."

"Be that as it may, Alonzo, your sorry face is just too well known, and you've stolen stuff from too many people. Including me. Don't think I don't know who dug them Canada geese out of my marsh!" Ferrus glowered at him.

Alonzo had the grace to duck his head in embarrassment. "I'm sorry about that. It was just too great a temptation with that decoy show in O.C. that weekend."

"If you get out of here and never, ever come back, I'll forgive you," Ferrus said, his tone begrudging.

"Well, I like the idea of stashing him on Jack Shepherd's boat," Desiree said. "Jack wants so much to know the local lore, this ought to be right up his alley."

And they were all looking at me again.

I swallowed the last of my beer. "Oh, no. Oh, no. I'm not gonna do this. I can't do this. I don't even know him all that well. Oh, no."

18

The Old Rugged Double Cross

Twilight arrives in earlier in late summer, hinting of colder days to come. The blue hour casts long shadows across the street, and somewhere behind a high privet hedge down the block and over, kids were playing softball; I could hear the crack of the bat and their excited voices. It was just the kind of summer evening I remembered as a kid, playing outside until the last possible moment, when Momma would call us in because it was getting too dark. Except now, here I was, all grown up and in deep, deep *e. coli.*

I looked around carefully before I opened the back of the van. "Come inside, and make it quick," I told Alonzo, who obediently hung into the shadows as he hightailed it up the back steps, across the porch, and into the house.

In front of me, Earlene had pulled into the driveway, cell phone in hand. She looked all around her as if she were certain that the police were lurking with drawn guns in the boxwood hedge.

I scurried up the back steps right behind them. Once inside, Earlene latched the screen door, probably the first time anyone's locked a door in Oysterback since maybe Word War II, when there was a rumor that the Nazis were offloading spies from submarines out in the Bay, or so Ferrus once told me. Why any self-respecting spy would want to come to Oysterback remains a mystery to me.

Of course, with an escaped convict rumored to be rolling around, there were probably a lot of locked doors today, even if the escapee was only Alonzo. But before Alonzo was an escaped convict, he'd steal anything that wasn't nailed down, and people still didn't lock their doors. Go figure.

I was getting a headache just thinking about it, and I knew exactly where Alonzo was; sitting down at the kitchen table, munching on some chocolate chip cookies that had come in while we were gone.

The good ladies of Devanau County had been playing elves and brownies while Earlene and I were out doing the devil's work. We both moaned in dismay at newly arrived corn pudding, tomato soup cake, and those aforementioned Toll House cookies.

"We've got to move on this *now!*" My sister greeted me with a wave of her phone. "Delmar just called and he, Wayne, and Momma are just leaving Miami."

"Then we need to get Alonzo long gone right this minute! I'm not entirely sure either Delmar or Wayne wants or needs this." I rubbed the palms of my hands against my pants. "And neither do we."

Earlene didn't reply; she was busy dialing up Dreedle's Funeral Home. "Parsons? I'm sorry to bother you over dinner, but Delmar just called and they're on their way home, so we can finally set a date. And frankly, the sooner the better . . ."

"I had no idea Miss Audrey had so many friends." Alonzo opened the refrigerator and poked around. He was right at home.

"Maybe they're glad she's passed over," I suggested nastily. "She was a threat to every marriage in three counties. Or at least she thought she was."

If I'd hoped that would get Earlene going, I was wrong. She just looked at me over her phone and shrugged, all the fight drained out of her.

"All right, thank you, Parsons. I knew we could count on you. Carrie and I will be over there tomorrow morning to discuss the arrangements." She shot me a look that meant I'd better come with her or else.

I stuck my head into the Florida room, but there was no sign of our star boarder. "I guess I'll have to go on down to the harbor and see if I can find him." I was dragging my feet and I knew it.

Earlene nodded. "Don't turn the lights on without drawing the shades. You-know-who is probably watching the house."

"Relax. They're probably going to be out there with the Rescue Squad and the fire trucks for hours. And you know Johnny Ray wouldn't miss a chance to boss everyone around and wave a flashlight."

"It's a guy thing—you wouldn't get it," Alonzo offered. "Got any milk to go with these here cookies?"

"For a man who broke out of a medium-security prison, you certainly are helpless," Earlene snapped. "The refrigerator is right over there, and I do believe you know where the glasses are kept." She turned back to me. "I don't guess you should waste any time tracking down Jack Shepherd. The sooner we get Alonzo out of here, the easier I'll breathe. Finding him here would be the last straw for Delmar."

"I just don't see why I have to ask him. Seems like Omar and Ferrus and Doreen and Desiree and *you* all know him better than I do."

"And they're all respectable people with something at stake. They all have businesses to run or people to answer to. Don't you think Doreen's kids would start to wonder where she was if she didn't come home? And Desiree's got the dinner rush and only Jack to help her. Omar's got the store and I have to get back . . ."

"I get it." I threw my hands up. "I'm the irresponsible hippie beatnik! I'm the only one with no fixed address or schedule! I'm the one who would harbor an escaped criminal, then try to drag someone I barely know into the, the . . . what? The *caper*? You all have been watching too much TV if you think this will work!"

"All of the above, Carrie. Besides that, he seems to like you."

I had to stand there with my mouth open. "Who figured that out? I met the man once. Or maybe twice."

"Oh, don't be silly. This is Oysterback. Everyone knows your business before you do. Miss Nettie knew both times I was pregnant, weeks before I even suspected. Just go and get him to take Alonzo off our hands. No one would look for him on Jack's boat. Jack's a foreigner, he's not from around here, so why would anyone think he'd be involved? Tell Jack this is his big chance to become a part of the story. That should convince him."

"An initiation. Why can't we just paddle him or something?"

"Because you can talk to Jack on his own intellectual level, so those two years of college didn't go to waste. You're so smart and sophisticated, you can think of what to say to convince him. And remember, we only have about six hours."

"It's stuff like this that made me leave town in the first place. Why in God's good name should I——"

Alonzo, finally sensing that he would have to fetch and carry his own milk, rose from the table with a gusty sigh and crossed the room.

"Some of us are getting really spoil——" I started to tell him, when Alonzo let out a shriek that rivaled the VFD fire siren.

"That's her! That's her!" He pointed to the window with a trembling finger.

Earlene and I turned to see the ghostly tower of Miss Carlotta Hackett's solidified blond hair, neatly framed by Momma's ruffled cherry-print curtains. And her eyes were as big as saucers.

"That's the blue-haired Conservative Christians lady I stole the gun from!" Alonzo screamed. "She's come to get me!"

"Or call Johnny Ray!" Earlene bolted for the door, almost pulling out the hook as she tore it open. "We've got to stop her!"

Well, a fat old lady with acrylic nails and big bleached hair can't move as fast as two premenopausal women, and it didn't take much for us to tackle her into the viburnum. It was sort of like two running backs tackling an elephant. This whole thing was getting much too physical for me. "I really have to stop smoking," I gasped as I fell across Miss Carlotta's legs.

"Harboring a criminal! I knew it! I knew it!" She was rolling around in the bushes, squealing and waving her cell phone while we struggled to hold her down. "I *told* Johnny Ray you were up to no good, Carrie Hudson! For shame, Earlene! You should know better! For shame on you!"

"I'd rather harbor a criminal than be one," Earlene panted as she yanked Miss Carlotta's phone out of her beringed hand. "Aren't you a little too old to be peeking in people's windows?"

"Yeah, I thought you had cable." I got a good sit on her rump, and Earlene pinned down her hands.

Miss Carlotta opened her mouth to scream and Earlene clapped her hand over that big lipliner'd orifice. I guess raising two hell monster boys taught my sister a lot about shutting people up.

"Well, now the whole town will know what we suspected all along: that you're a peeping Tom." Earlene was breathing hard.

"Or a peeping Thomasina," I said hysterically.

"And the ones that don't know, well, I'll tell them all," Earlene grunted. "Shame on you! And at your age, Miss Carlotta.

Crawling around in the bushes and lookin' in people's windows!"

"Mmmmmpf!"

"Carrie, get the duct tape out of the kitchen drawer," my sister commanded me. "Miss Carlotta is going into cold storage until we're sure Alonzo's gotten out of Dodge."

"Mmmmpf!"

"And don't forget a scarf! We can't have her screaming her head off!"

"Yes, *ma'am*!"

Even with the windows open and a breeze flushing through the cab, the night air was as thick and black as raspberry jam. The town seemed deserted; either folks were at home, hunkered down in the air-conditioning, or out on Route 50 staring at blood and twisted metal. When I drove past the fire department, all the doors were up and the lights were blazing, but there was neither a ladder truck nor a human in sight.

"Carrie, there's something I need to tell you," my sister said, sitting beside me in the darkness.

"Tell away."

"It's about those boxes I took out of the house. I know everyone told you I was taking Momma's stuff, but that wasn't it. I packed up all your baby albums and report cards and high school yearbooks and stuff Momma'd saved over the years. Your baby booties, your high school diploma. Your debate team trophy."

"God, Earlene, why would you want to save that old stuff? It's all crap. I would have thrown it out. No, I would have built a bonfire and danced around it like a witch."

"Aren't you the sentimental one," Alonzo offered.

"Shut up," we both said at once.

"That's why I saved it. Because I knew you'd want to throw it all out. I thought that someday you'd miss all that stuff and wish you had it back. Maybe the time will come when you'll be in the mood to look at it, and try to figure out how you got to where you are and where you're going. You've been lost too long. You've got to find some peace."

I glanced at my sister's thin profile in the darkness. I thought she was going to tell me I had to come home to Jesus, but she surprised me.

"If you can put the past behind you," Earlene continued slowly, "you can make a bonfire out of all of that stuff and dance around it stark naked for all I care. But I just hope that you'll stop running away one of these days. Maybe start running toward something?"

It was on my mind to make some sarcastic remark about psychobabble, but then I realized what she was trying to tell me, and if we hadn't been in such desperate, dramatic, stupid straits, I would have burst into tears. Earlene was reaching out.

"Awww," Alonzo cooed.

"Shut up," my sister and I told him again as we bounced down the rutted road to the harbor.

Mosquitoes buzzed around my head as I reluctantly parked the van alongside Jack's slip in the harbor. In the crepuscular light, it all looked romantic, with the moon dancing on the tide and the ghostly white shapes bobbing quietly in their slips. There was a dim light in the galley of the Triton.

"You wait here," I told Alonzo as I slid out of the van. "Don't let him go anywhere, Earlene."

"I won't move," he promised, but I knew his bond was as firm as a snowball in hell; Alonzo was a travelin' man. Earlene's grip on his arm was my best insurance.

HELEN CHAPPELL

Wondering how the hell I got into this mess, I edged
unsteadily out on the catwalk beside Jack's boat, calling his
name. If he was gone for the evening, we were in deep doo-doo.

But for once in my misbegotten life, luck was with me.

"Hey, Carrie." Jack's head was thrust through the hatchway,
and he was smiling, which was a good sign. "I just opened a bottle of wine. Would you like a glass of . . . What happened? You
look as if you'd seen a ghost." His smile fell away.

Without waiting for permission, I boarded. "Listen, Jack,
you say you want to experience all there is to experience about
Oysterback, right? Well, do I have an opportunity for you!"

He had the grace to look interested. I swung through the
hatch and into the galley. The queen of the low-enders was
about to deliver the sales pitch of her life.

And it wasn't easy in that tiny galley. Even with the pull-
down table between us, Jack was only inches away. I could have
reached out and touched that distracting hint of chest hair. But
there was business at hand and here I was begging for the
biggest favor in the world.

It was a long, sad, and very convoluted tale that required a lot
of explaining and backstory and multiple biographies and in
the end, confessions of stuff I rarely tell anyone. I did my best,
but it was hard to tell how it was going down. Jack just sat there
under the propane lantern, his plastic wineglass in hand, smiling at me as if I were telling the longest shaggy-dog story in the
history of the world. He didn't even seem too offended when I
told him I'd been laboring under the suspicion that he and
Momma were More Than Friends.

"This will make you one of us forever," I promised. "It's better than the key to the city. You do this and you're a part of this
town for the rest of your life." I knew that appeal would either
hook him or scare him to death, but hey, desperate times
require desperate measures. "The only thing is, you have to do

it now, before my brother-in-law and my brother get back. Otherwise, it will never work. You don't know what Delmar's like. He's such a straight arrow, he'll call the cops himself." As a final inducement, I brought out the roll of cash I'd gained from my trip to Rehobeth. "I know you don't have time to provision or anything, but if you can just get out of here tonight, and maybe even gunk-hole somewhere down the Bay overnight and start out in the morning . . ."

But Jack just laughed. "Put your money away, sailor. It's no good here, as Desiree says." He leaned forward and actually put his hand over mine, forcing my cash stash away from him. I noticed that he didn't take his hand away, either, and then I noticed that I sort of liked that. Danger *is* an aphrodisiac.

"You want me to take Audrey's escaped-con boyfriend off to Florida in my boat, down the Inland Waterway, and you want me to do it tonight. You want me just to leave Oysterback without a word to anyone."

"We want you to go while the going's good. I don't think we tied and gagged Miss Carlotta all that well. I mean she's got arthritis and stuff, so we'll have to let her out soon. But you need to hoist anchor and blow town before everyone else gets back from the accident."

"And *we* is"—he counted on his fingers—"Doreen, Desiree, Ferrus, Omar, and Earlene. That's probably more people than were in on the Kennedy assassination conspiracy."

"And me," I added. "I'm in on it too. And now, so are you. We've got to get him away from here before he has to go back to jail and gets everyone in trouble. He's not the brightest bulb on the string, you know, but he's *our* bulb." I swallowed hard. "And now, he's your bulb too. You wanted the ultimate Oysterback scoop. Now you can be part of it."

"And this escapade is going to stay secret?" He looked very dubious, but I could tell he really wanted to laugh. At that point, I was beyond humor. Being in a whole world of trouble focuses your mind wonderfully.

"This is a town that knows how to keep its secrets. To this day, no one knows the Boone brothers are out on the marsh except us."

"The Boone brothers?"

"It's a long story," I said quickly. "But take Alonzo to Florida and steer him toward Key West where my brother, Wayne, lives, and when you come back from the islands in the spring, we'll—" I shuddered. "We'll actually take you out there so you can meet the Boones for yourself." Talk about the supreme sacrifice.

"I don't know," Jack said with a smile. He leaned back against the cushions. "This sounds risky to me."

"But it's for Momma. For Audrey. We're all doing this for her, not Alonzo. You're acting like this is a joke, but it's not a joke to us."

Then he looked thoughtful for a while. I was trying to figure out what to do next when he set his glass down on the table. "Okay, I'll do it for Audrey. It beats wearing a chicken suit," he announced. "Now, let's meet the man who's caused everyone so much trouble. You swear he's not violent, right?"

"No, as I said, he's not a brain trust, but he's not violent," I promised. I felt an enormous sense of having something limp and gray and heavy removed from my solar plexus, as if a great weight had been removed from my spirit.

Jack stood up, filling the tiny galley. "But I just want *you* to know one thing: I'm doing this for *you*, not for your mother, not for the town, okay?"

All I could do was nod before I got the kiss of my life. And I mean that man could kiss. A red-hot *frisson* traveled through my body and went right down into my toes before he let go of me. And right away, I wished he'd do it again. Oh, yes, he could kiss.

"We'll get back to that later." Jack was breathing heavily. "But for now, there's business at hand."

Outside, Earlene was standing by the van, her hand firmly attached to Alonzo's arm. When she saw Jack and me emerge from the boat, all she had to do was look at Jack's grin to know that the professorial genie had granted our three wishes. Or at least one of them.

"Hi, Earlene!" Jack strolled across the parking lot to greet her, as if this were just a Saturday-night six-pack blast. "This your friend I'm taking far and away?"

Jack solemnly shook Alonzo's hand and commented on his hair, which he said he liked.

"You know anything about boats?"

Alonzo puffed out his scrawny chest. "I been on the water all my life," he said proudly.

Neither Earlene nor I thought this was the time to mention he'd been *stealing* off the water all his life.

They were still feeling each other out, as men will do, when I saw the headlights bouncing down the road. "Stay in the shadows," I commanded. "We might be busted."

But it was Doreen's Grand Cherokee. As we watched, Doreen, Desiree, Ferrus, and Omar climbed down from the SUV. Each one was bearing bags and sacks. For a minute, I thought they had all decided to run away with Jack, leave their Oysterback lives far behind to become some other people in some other place. I knew, given a choice right then, that's what I would do.

"We thought you'd need some provisions," Desiree said, opening the hatch to reveal several bags of ice. "I brought some booze and ice and some of Earl Don's clothes, so Alonzo would have something to wear."

"I packed up some odds and ends of soap and shampoo samples from the salon, and got some of Junie's foul-weather gear.

It'll be swimming on you, Alonzo, but Junie's got so much stuff, he'll never notice. Or he'll think the boys took it and lost it somewhere. And some towels and a sleeping bag." Doreen was nothing if not practical.

"Groceries," Omar said shortly, grunting as he offloaded boxes of food. "You got to have something to eat, so I took some stuff from my store. Lots of instant stuff. And water. I got about six two-ten jugs of water here. That ought to hold you 'til you get to a marina down the Bay."

Ferrus seemed to be empty-handed, but he reached into his pocket and held up a key ring. "I can open the marina gas pumps." He winked. "No sense leavin' without a full tank of fuel."

It occurred to me that they knew Jack better than I did. There had never been any doubt in their minds that he would fall in with the plan. They knew his price: he wanted to be an Oysterback insider, and this was the ultimate town caper, something they'd talk about for years to come.

"I guess you are one of us already," I told the professor softly.

Jack just kept on grinning. He picked up two big bags of ice. "I guess we'd better get this stuff on board if we're shoving off tonight. High tide's in about an hour."

"Take these boots, Carrie," Doreen told me. She was holding her wallet in her teeth, so she sounded funny. Omar, Jack, and Ferrus had already formed a chain to convey the goodies into the boat. Jack had hopped aboard, and was stowing ice below.

"Alonzo, give me a hand," Earlene said, taking plastic sacks of groceries from the Jeep. "Alonzo? Drat the man, where is he now?" Suddenly, the plastic sacks slid from her hands. "Nooooo!" she breathed.

Alonzo was opening the back door of my van.

"I'm just going to get them Snickers bars," he said, pulling the handles open.

"Alonzo! No!"

He pulled back the doors, pushing himself up into the van.

The shotgun blast was so loud that it hurt my ears, echoing through the hollow harbor.

Slowly, Alonzo took a step back. But there was nothing to step on but air, and he slowly crumpled onto the asphalt.

He lay on his back, making a horrible wheezing sound, his wide-eyed expression that of a man who has been sadly disappointed.

One rattling breath, and I just knew he was dead.

Tower of hair askew, bits and pieces of duct tape still clinging to her animal print polyester blouse, Miss Carlotta Hackett stood just inside my van, right where Earlene and I had stashed her. In one hand, she was clutching my 28-gauge Handi Gun. The sawed-off barrel was still smoking. She must have been on top of Alonzo when she pulled the trigger.

Pieces fell into place. After Earlene and I had wrestled her into the van, she'd gotten loose and found my gun under the futon. The goddamned gun.

Miss Carlotta looked around at all of us, but her eyes weren't seeing; they were as vacant as Alonzo's.

"He opened the doors and I knew he was going to kill me," she wailed, then burst into tears.

The aftershock from the shotgun blast echoed against the boats, the bulkheads, and the water, repeating itself far across the river against the distant shore.

Alonzo opened one eye. "Am I dead yet?" His voice was plaintive as he scanned our anxious faces looking down at him.

"Hell, no!" Ferrus rumbled, furiously picking tiny pieces of .28 shot out of his arm. "Goddammit, Carlotta, when you shoot a gun at someone, take aim! You couldn't hit the broad side of a barn, door, but you just nipped my carving arm with that cannon! It'll take me an hour to dig out them damn pellets!"

Miss Carlotta took one look at Alonzo, who had not so much as a scratch on him, and swooned right off the truck.

If he hadn't been lying there to break her fall, she might have hurt herself.

"Get her off! She's killin' me!" Oysterback's favorite criminal cried, very much alive.

19

Mint Condition and in the Original Box

"What were those little camera things beside the coffin for?" I heard someone in the kitchen behind me whisper. "Was the funeral on TV or something?"

"Oh, that's for the brother. He won't go around large crowds, so he had Delmar wire some kind of video thing with the funeral service to his computer and he watched it back here at Audrey's house. He's some kind of crazy genius or something."

Or something, I thought. Typical Wayne. While the rest of us sat in the front pew of Oysterback United Methodist, piously facing the urn, he was hiding out in his old room at home, watching the action on his laptop. Packs of people make him nervous, he said. Wayne was still different. He was born different and he'd die different.

"He should have gone through what we went through. Now *that* would make him nervous." That was Earlene's pronouncement. But both of us knew that once Wayne had made up his mind, he wouldn't budge. Wayne and his computer had barely come out of his room since he and Delmar had rolled in. Earlene said if we wanted to talk to him, we should send him an e-mail.

"Besides, what if Johnny Ray shows up?" my sister had added. "He thinks Alonzo is Wayne. Better this way, right?"

As I sat at the service, I wondered how Daddy would feel about Momma's escapades and decided he probably wouldn't care, since he thought whatever Momma did was just fine. I could barely remember him, he'd been dead so long, and so invisible when he was alive. He spent more time in town at his law offices than he ever did at home, and if truth be told, he wasn't very good at his job. Nevertheless, he devoted himself to his clients, the poor and the disenfranchised and the, God knows, guilty as sin. Who else would hire Daddy for a lawyer around here except those who could afford no one better? Would things have been different if he'd survived the heart attack he'd had while waiting for Momma outside the Salon de Beauté? Of course. The men, for instance. Momma never would have gotten involved with all of them if Daddy were still around. But I was tired of playing what if, should have, could have. Things were what they were, and nothing could change the past.

That was my new attitude and I was clinging to it as if it were a rock in a stormy sea.

No one had to say anything about keeping quiet about Alonzo. You live around here long enough, you learn not to put your business out on the street for outsiders to pick over, just as you learn not to write any checks with your mouth that your ass can't cash.

"I wonder why Carlotta Hackett didn't come. She was next-door neighbors with Audrey for years and years," a woman in the kitchen said. "And she dearly loves a funeral."

"I heard she had a nervous spell and went off to visit with her sister in Arbutus for a while," a companion informed her.

Well, that much was true. For someone who was an outstanding light in the Conservative Christians Central Committee's Second Amendment Coalition, Miss Carlotta was awfully sensitive about having almost gunned down an escaped convict in lukewarm blood. I guess she was a weak Second Amendment Sister.

Neither Earlene nor I could find it in our hearts to hold her attempt at killing Alonzo against her. After all, it was sort of our fault, for having bound, gagged, and kidnapped her. But if she hadn't been a peeper, she wouldn't have put herself in that position in the first place. If only, if only, if only.

In the end, if Momma hadn't gotten involved with Alonzo, none of this would have happened. He was the most hapless human being I'd ever met in my life, and except for an old lady's bad aim, he would have been dead meat. Since I was almost responsible for killing him, I knew I was going to have to think long and hard to come to terms with that idea.

My Handi Gun was at the bottom of Jack's Hole, way out in the Bay, quietly rusting away under three hundred feet of water. I didn't want it back; I didn't want a gun that almost killed a human being, no matter how antique it was.

Out of the corner of my eye, I saw Delmar and Earlene come around the house and sink into the lawn chairs beneath the shade of the big old pin oak in the backyard. Delmar looked so dorky in his short-sleeved rayon shirt and wide black necktie. I reminded myself that I was going to be more respectful of him from now on in. He had more courage than I did, going down to Florida and dealing with crazy Wayne. That and knowing now how he had defended me against Chester the Molester.

Earlene and Delmar had no idea I was watching them as they smiled at each other with the sort of unspoken communication that says everything without words. It was so easy to tell that these were two people who were comfortable together, who had hewn out a bond. In that moment I realized the love between them had allowed them to survive a lot of bad times and given them a lot of good times. Just by the way Delmar slipped his arm along the back of Earlene's chair and she leaned into him, the two of them smiling, you could tell this was true love. Theirs was the kind of commitment that doesn't need dramas and heartaches and upsets to prove its worth, but is something calming and secure.

So that was what it was, love that lasts. Understanding the other person well enough to accept them for what they were as much as for what they weren't. That, I thought, is what I want for myself, if I ever get a chance.

I wondered what would happen if I opened myself up to that idea. Thinking about Jack Shepherd, and the possibilities of him, I wasn't anxious or afraid. Either it would happen or it wouldn't. But I sure hoped it would. If I'd thought he was a great kisser the first time, that last kiss, before he and Alonzo cast off for the islands and parts unknown, convinced me there was something to be explored. And judging from his e-mails, he felt the same way.

For the first time in a long time, I pondered what could happen, and for the first time in a long time, the future didn't seem all that chained to the past. If I get a chance for love this time, I thought, I will not drive it away. I am only responsible for my own happiness.

"Carrie, do you know where the toilet paper is?" Desiree stuck her head out the door.

"I'll get it," I said, and went back to being a hostess at a wake.

Momma would have been pleased.

20

I Got Them
Old Bay Blues Again

Across the long purple shadows falling over the marsh, I heard the calling of a Canada goose. First one, then another. The first geese of fall had arrived early this year, but they brought with them the promise of a new season.

"Until I saw that clod of dirt hit that coffin, I couldn't breathe. Give me one of those cigarettes, then promise me you'll stop smoking." Earlene sank down on the glider next to me and kicked off her black pumps. She smoothed the skirt of her black suit down and leaned back. "Is that a goose I hear? Autumn's not far away now. Momma used to say, the older you get, the faster the time goes. Now I know what she meant. Seems as if summer just started a week or two ago."

I handed her the pack and my lighter. "So, how do you think it all went?"

"Pretty well. We had to set out a third platter of ham and we're out of snowflake rolls, and just about everything else is picked to crumbs. Where did you disappear to at the end?"

"I just ducked out for a minute. Miss Nettie had me cornered behind the buffet table with pictures of her grandchildren. Pretty good turnout, huh?"

"You can't say that Momma didn't have a lot of friends.

There were people here I haven't seen in years. I didn't think so many of them would come back to the house after the burial, but Doreen said it looks like we had around a hundred people all together."

"At least we fed them before we blessed them and sent them on their way."

I looked down at my own plate, where I was balancing the remains of ham, turkey, stringbean casserole, corn pudding, sweet potato casserole, and cole slaw. "They can say we laid out a good spread. Now we have all those dishes to wash and return. Plus we have to replace the ones we broke. And each one gets a thank-you note!"

"Momma would have loved this." Earlene inhaled deeply and slowly blew the smoke out, watching it roll in the air in front of her. "She would have adored all the attention."

The house was quiet now. It seemed odd, after so much clamor, but the last mourners were gone, and it was just the family now. Earlene's boys were watching TV, two big lugs sprawled out in the living room in front of ESPN.

"I can't believe all the people who have come up to me with a story to share about Momma. But if one more old lady asked me when I'm getting married and settling down, I think I would have puked."

Earlene glanced at her watch. "At their time of life, all the entertainment a lot of these people get is the satisfaction of see-ing other people die before they do. Good Lord, Reverend Briscoe told me old Mrs. Gunderson pestered her teenage grandson until he took her out of the nursing home and brought her down here. She had the time of her life—she told me so on her way out."

"Of course, half the people she was talking to have been dead for thirty years."

Earlene sipped at her iced tea, pinky finger extended. "Careful. We'll probably be the same way when we're old ladies."

"Not me! I want to die young, shot by a jealous wife. It will add to my legend."

She shot me a look but said nothing for a minute, tapping her ashes off into the geraniums.

"With all the mess with Al—with everything that's been going on, I mean"—she corrected herself swiftly, with a look around, because you never knew who was listening—"I never did get to talk to you about Momma's will."

"I don't want anything, Earlene. You deserve it all—you take it. I'll just end up blowing anything I get, or giving it to Greenpeace or even to a home for stray cats. I can feel myself headed that way now. In ten years or so, I'll be a crazy old lady, pushing a shopping cart and talking to myself and opening cans of Super Supper in alleyways."

All of a sudden, that didn't seem so funny. Or so far-fetched. I shivered.

"That's what you say now, but when you're older and looking to settle down, you'll be glad you have something to fall back on. You're not getting any younger, and neither am I. And God knows, Wayne will probably always need to have his money managed."

We both looked toward the edge of the yard, down by the marsh, where Delmar was fussing over what looked like a cell phone with a computer monitor and a lot of wires and antennas. No doubt some invention of Wayne's they were testing. It crackled every now and then, loudly enough to be heard back up at the house.

Up in his room, Wayne called instructions down to Delmar. He still hadn't come out, not all afternoon. Not that I blamed him. Earlene and I felt it made perfect sense. In spite of the fact that he lived in the Keys, Wayne was as pale as a ghost and as antisocial as ever.

"Anyway"—Earlene's voice came out in a rush—"the will is pretty basic. Wayne and I each get some stocks and bonds, some of Momma's stuff." She took a deep breath. "And you get the house."

"Oh, no. Oh, no! Momma reaches out from beyond the grave! I don't want the house. It's not fair to you and Wayne."

Earlene shook her head. "Actually, Carrie, you're coming out on the short end of the deal. Momma was a very shrewd investor, although you'd never know it by the way she lived in this place, the way she nickel and dimed everything in sight. Wayne and I are in pretty good shape. Or we will be, after probate."

"I wonder how much a bungalow on the marsh is worth to city folk," I mused. "Enough to buy a new van?"

"It needs some work, Delmar says. He was always after Momma to remodel the kitchen and the bathroom, and to look after the sills for posthole beetle damage."

"I don't know. A house, *this house*! It's just her way of trying to anchor me to this town! That is so Momma! I don't want the responsibility! I like my freedom!"

"Well, you could sell it and buy something else. But . . ."

"But what, Earlene? I can practically hear your wheels turning."

She pressed her knees together, lacing her manicured fingers in her lap, examining her rings as if they were new. "Actually, I was hoping you'd stay around here, for a while at least. We'll have to sort out all of Momma's stuff, and you know what a pack rat she was, and I don't want to do that alone. I need you to make decisions because you know what's worth what. I don't know anything about old stuff."

"We may as well just get a Dumpster and shovel. She was a

one-woman version of the Collier brothers, you know, those two crazy old men in New York, the ones who died and left that whole apartment full of old junk and newspapers they'd accumulated over the years?"

"Oh, no! She did recycle!" Earlene assured me, then laughed. She placed a cool hand on top of mine. "This is hard to say, because I have no tact and you're as touchy as a June bug, but, Carrie, I was hoping you'd stay around for a while so we could, I don't know . . . How do I say this?" She seemed to be asking her hands this question. Then she looked at me. "Don't make this harder than it is, Carrie. We're not a great family for spilling our feelings, but for once I'd like to try. After everything we've been through in the past couple of days, it just seems that when we actually try and work together, we do pretty well, you and I."

I took a deep breath. "Wow, Earlene. It's on the tip of my tongue to say something smart, this kind of knee-jerk reaction, and *I'm not doing it!* I'm not doing it! This is so cool! Does this mean I'm finally growing up?" I was making fun of myself, but it was true. For once in my life, I wasn't being a smartass. Amazingly, it was not a bad feeling. "And I guess in a way, we're all we've got. Aw, Jeez, Earlene, don't cry!"

She straightened her spine. "I'm not crying," she sniffed. "I'm not a drama queen."

"No," I agreed, "you're not. You've been really great. You handled Alonzo and everything with a lot more courage than I did. And a lot more imagination. I loved it when you stood up to Johnny Ray over at Doreen's. You were wonderful!"

"Was I?" My sister looked pleased with herself.

"You were *majestic*. You've done things I never thought I would ever see you do. We've had an adventure, Earlene. We cleaned up Momma's last mess and came out on the other side!"

"Yes, I guess I did do okay. But you know, I couldn't have

done it without you. If Alonzo'd turned up and you weren't here, I don't know what I would have done. Messed things up even more, probably. Made a huge scandal."

"But we did it. We did it! Do you realize that we actually pulled it off?" We both giggled.

Delmar looked up from his wires and computers and waved. We returned the wave and he went back to fooling with Wayne's latest invention, shaking his head the whole time. I had a feeling it was going to take him a while to figure out this new sisterly configuration. Of course, it was going to take us a while, too. Unlike Momma, some things aren't easy to bury. But like burying Momma, you can try.

"This is important to me," Earlene said quietly.

"Then it's important to me, too."

"Besides," Earlene said, laughing, "think about how clearing all this junk out of here will save us tons of money in therapy bills."

"You've got a point." I bit my lip. "Okay, I'll stay around and we'll clean this place out. And after that, we'll just have to see." I sat quietly for a moment. "It's not as bad being back here as I thought it would be," I admitted.

We sat for a moment and I thought about life on the road. The traffic, the living out of the van, the endless series of cheap motels and truck stops and gas stations. The weird situations, the weirder people. A couple of days ago, it seemed glamorous and exciting. Now, the idea of not having to drive, of having a real bath and a real toilet and a real kitchen and a real bed, all of that seemed appealing.

How many times, driving miles and miles at night, had I passed a house and through a window caught a fleeting glimpse of the life within? Had I ever wished I was living there? Could I try living like a civilian again, like a normal person, for even a little while? Would I miss the fast-food joints and the thrill of the next auction, the tag sale just over the hill? Could I stand belonging somewhere, belonging with someone? For a moment, I thought about gathering up all my stuff, jumping in my van, and driving away, never to return.

The prospect didn't feel as good as I thought it might, not anymore. I was tired of running. Especially now that I realized that all the things I had been running from had been riding along with me all the time. Wherever I went, there they were. Maybe it really was time to stop running, and to try something new, like settling down and becoming a civilian.

"You know," Earlene offered, "there's an empty storefront where the old gas station was. It would make a great antique store."

"Mae West once said, when faced with two evils, always chose the one you've never tried before." I frowned. "I could stock it out of this house, you know. Get a permanent address, pay taxes like a real citizen. Maybe start going to church and attending town meetings."

"Don't get carried away," Earlene said wisely. "We both have been guilty in the past of trying to swallow the whole pie before we even know if we liked the taste of it. From now on, let's just start with a little bite. We'll save ourselves a lot of indigestion that way." She turned to me and put out her hand. "Deal?"

"Deal."